A BATTLE FOR TOMORROW

END OF EARTH, BOOK 1

MATT SIMONS

Development Editing by Maureen Simons
Editing by The Pro Book Editor
Interior and Cover Design by IAPS.rocks

eBook ISBN: 978-1-7378665-0-3
paperback ISBN: 978-1-7378665-1-0

  1. Main category—Science Fiction/Time Travel
  2. Other category—War & Military
  3. Other category—Thrillers

First Edition

CHAPTER 1

'VE ALWAYS BEEN BAD AT taking tests. It took me three years to pass the school district's standardized testing while everyone else passed it freshman year. I just have a hard time memorizing, especially when it comes to math. I can't remember formulas to save my life. I excel on all the homework because I have all the formulas right next to me, but the instant I have to go off memory, I end up forgetting a minus sign or a decimal point. But this time, I came prepared. I have every formula I need written on my forearm, carefully hidden with a long-sleeved shirt. As long as I write out each problem, Ms. Fowler won't notice.

Only a few minutes into the test, someone's phone goes off, sounding like an alarm. Who uses that for their ringtone?

"I thought I told all of you to turn your phones off during the test!" Ms. Fowler says to the class.

Wow, Ms. Fowler is pissed.

The scared kid insists he did, but she rips his test away, saying, "I told all of you, if your phone goes off during the test, I will assume you are cheating and you will fail this final!"

I cover my arm. She's such a Nazi when it comes to phones in class. I always keep mine silent at school. I am not going down because of some telemarketer.

Then another kid's phone goes off with the same alert.

Ms. Fowler starts yelling at the new victim. "What is wrong with all of you? Do you not respect me this much?"

The end of the first semester is really getting to her. Maybe it's the cold weather, made worse inside because the AC never turns off.

Then my phone starts buzzing. What the heck? Mine was definitely silent. Everyone's phone is sounding off the same alert. Even Ms. Fowler's phone sounds off from her desk. Ok, this is kind of spooky.

I look down at my phone and read what appears to be a nationwide alert statement. "Attention. Hawaii has been impacted with a nuclear warhead."

Bullshit, is this some kind of fucked up senior prank? "Ms. Fowler, look at your phone! I think we have a bigger issue than the test."

Everyone starts freaking out.

"What do we do?"

"Is this the end of the world?"

"This can't be real."

Then Ms. Fowler exclaims, "Enough! Everyone calm down!"

Everyone stops and stares at Ms. Fowler. What do we do?

The loudspeaker comes on with Vice Principal Harrison's gravelly voice made worse through the old intercom speakers. "Attention, students. Please follow your teachers in an orderly manner to the fallout shelter."

This is real. Oh my god, this is actually happening. Am I going to die? Are we all going to die? Is this the end? There's so much I wanted to do. I never got to touch a boob.

Ms. Fowler tells everyone, "Grab your things and form a line."

I want to run as fast as I can to the fallout shelter. I bet I could get there in less than a minute, but I don't know where the shelter is. So I follow the line.

The mass of students moves slower than I would like. At any moment the next shoe could drop. Then I see the entrance to the bunker is under the auditorium. Teachers wave us through, doing their best to keep students calm and moving. I am so happy that our high school was built during the cold war.

The bunker is large, but not large enough. It was clearly designed for a smaller population. It looks like an empty cafeteria two stories underground. There are no chairs anywhere. The ground is so dusty, clearly no one has been in here in a long time. Each step kicks dust into the air, causing people to cough and sneeze uncontrollably.

Teachers take role to be sure we're not leaving anyone behind and then the vault door closes with an ominous lock. Everyone falls silent. Everyone is scared. I can feel the tension. I feel claustrophobic, like I can't breathe right. I'm squeezed between all my classmates. The mass of body heat is slowly cooking me. Someone turn on the air-conditioning, please.

Silence grips us for an hour. Someone is squeezing my arm. I look behind me to see the popular Amy clutching my arm tightly. She's always been popular. Always surrounded by the most beautiful people in our grade, but none are to be found in Ms. Fowler's College Algebra. I've known her since elementary school. I thought I was invisible to her. Her grip is so tight it kind of hurts. What should I do?

This could be my chance with her. I put my hand over her hand and whisper, "We're going to be fine. These bunkers were designed for days like today."

Her grip relaxes a bit.

I take my hand away, hiding my fear behind a smile.

I know how this ends. I've seen the movies. If I say any more, I will either creep her out or just embarrass myself and before I know it, everyone will be laughing at me. Or worse, her current boyfriend on the football team will beat the crap out of me. I turn away, but she doesn't let go.

By hour two, people start to mingle and try to find their friend groups. The teachers and staff start patrolling to keep students in line. I think they know if they're too strict in this small environment, they could face a riot.

Amy whispers a quiet, "Thank you," as she leaves to go find her group.

That is the most she's ever said to me. Should I have tried to talk to her? What if she always thought she was invisible to *me*? For so long I've viewed her as someone out of my league that I've never even tried to talk to her. Could she actually have the smallest of crushes on me?

She finds her boyfriend, and they embrace and kiss with a passion I don't have. That answers that question.

I don't have any friends in this class. I scan the sea of faces for the only student with a large blond Afro and glasses. My best friend Rick, who stands out in any crowd.

He will also be near Alex, the tallest student in our class. He easily stands a solid foot above all the teachers. Their second period was AP Chemistry, so they should be near each other.

There they are sitting against one of the walls. Rick is mid conversation with Zack, the silver-haired comic. Where's Alex? He should be near and easy to spot. Whatever. I can find him later.

"Hey, guys." I bump knuckles with Rick and Zack.

"Hey, Jason," Rick replies.

Zack is the shortest of us. I met him and Alex in middle school. Rick, Zack, Alex, and I built an alliance to survive middle school PE. We weren't the strongest, so we had to use our wits. Alex has the height, Zack has the speed, Rick has the brains, and I have the endurance to keep going long after most slow down.

"We were just discussing the possible end of the world. Care to join us?" Zack's voice cracks more than normal. Normally there would be a joke about it, but not this time.

"Sure, not much else to do. Where's Alex?"

Zack points to the left where Alex is sitting on the ground, talking to Katie. The only one of us with a girlfriend.

I make eye contact, and he nods at me.

Rick says, "They've been huddled together this whole time. Lost in each other."

Katie doesn't really like us. When she gets her way, Alex might as well be on the moon. I ask if their phones have any service.

Rick replies, "No, there's too much concrete between us and the surface."

Zack says, "And the possible end of the world could be jamming up people's signals. There might be one of those old spin dial phones somewhere." He stands up and looks around excitedly.

Rick asks, "How bad was the math test?"

I make sure my sleeve is still covering my arm. "It wasn't easy, but I have a feeling that it doesn't matter anymore."

Zack bumps me rather hard. "No need to bring down the already down mood, dude."

"Any sign of that spin dial phone?"

"No. Did you guys have any plans for the holiday vacation?" Zack says, doing his best to keep this conversation going.

Rick answers faster than me, "My family was going to come into town for Hanukkah. But plans might change."

"How about a game?" Zack pulls out a rather dirty, folded paper triangle from his bag.

"Good idea." Rick shakes his head in approval.

I have to ask, "How long has that been in there?"

"About a year. I don't know how to fold them, so I keep one on me at all times."

To play paper football, one must flick the paper triangle at their opponent while they hold up their fingers like a field goal. However, our paper football is bent and dirty, so it doesn't fly quite right.

"More challenge means more fun," says Zack.

This kills another hour. We lose every round to Rick.

On the fiftieth consecutive victory, I ask, "How do you do that?"

"Do what?" he answers with a smirk as he flicks the triangle directly through my fingers.

"That. How do you never miss?"

He says, "I'm just amazing."

"Bullshit." I flick the football hard at his face but miss and it flies past his afro.

"What the fuck!"

Shit, who did I hit?

A large hulking figure rises behind Rick.

Of course, I had to hit the superstar athlete Dylan. There's a rumor going around that he's on steroids. It makes sense with how quick to anger he is, but I've known this beast since middle school and he's always been a jerk. Now I just gave him an excuse to be angry in this confined space. Shit.

His eyes burn with rage. "Which one of you little shits threw this at me?"

I stutter, "S-s-sorry, Dylan. Didn't mean to hit you." I can't hide the fear in my voice.

Alex stops his talk with Katie and stands in front of me. He is the only one of us taller than the angry mass of muscle known as Dylan. However, Alex doesn't have nearly the muscle mass as Dylan. Plus, Dylan has his crew by him at all times and they outnumber us by five. The football linemen never travel alone.

Dylan crushes the paper football in his hand. He looks ready to kill as he steps forward. It feels like the ground shakes with each step.

I have to talk my way out of this. Come on, think.

Then he stops his advance, but the rage doesn't leave his eyes. "I'll kill you later."

They sit back down and proceed to talk shit about us, like we can't hear them.

Why didn't he do anything? A simple threat is not like him. I look behind me and there stands the PE teacher and assistant football coach, Linda Payne, a former Olympic weightlifter until she had kids. She is the most imposing middle-aged woman on Earth. Christ, I always forget how buff she is. She may not be an Olympian anymore, but she clearly never stopped training.

Zack asks, "Does anyone else need to use a bathroom?"

I say, "I didn't, but now I kind of need to."

After five hours, the bunker doors open and we are dismissed. I've never needed to piss so badly in my life. The world is still in one piece. Was it all just a prank?

Everyone's phones sound off with important news bulletins and phone calls from parents and loved ones. No, it was real. Hawaii is gone. Well, at least the big island is, and the United Nations called an emergency meeting. I have ten voice mails from Mom and three from Dad.

I call Dad first, thinking he's less likely to freak out. "Jason! Where are you? Why didn't you answer? Your mom is worried sick."

Or I could have been wrong. "The school put us in the fallout bunker. I didn't have reception underground."

He calms down a bit. "Ok, I'm glad you're safe. Just come home."

"I'm leaving school now. Any word from Pete or Ann?"

"They're both fine. Pete was too busy studying to know what was going on. That boy just *had* to pick law school."

"And how's Ann?"

"Your sister, on the other hand, has been freaking out. Which only added to your mother's panic. It took a while, but I finally got them to calm down."

I should talk to my older siblings more, but Pete's in grad school and Ann's trying to figure out her college path.

Dad asks, "Hey, I went to that school when it first opened and never got to see the bunker. What was it like?"

"Like an empty cafeteria several stories underground."

He asks, "Were there any bathrooms?"

"There was one and the line formed around the entire room. I decided to wait till they let us out, figuring it was about the same wait time."

He laughs. "Remember, toilet paper will hold value in any apocalypse."

"I know, Dad. What would you guys do for cold war drills, if you didn't go to the bunker?"

Dad says, "We would duck and cover, but when I got to high school, we realized that hiding under our desks probably wouldn't help. I'll tell your mother you're fine. We're both home."

"I'll be home in a bit."

"Ok, drive safe. It's pandemonium out there." He sounded calm. Almost too calm. He's trying to act strong. That man never shows fear. He'll always show humor first.

"I will." And I hang up.

I go to the men's restroom on the second floor of the third building since it rarely gets traffic during normal school hours, giving me privacy while the rest of the student body crowd the bathrooms closest to the bunker. Then I went to my car. At the center of the parking lot stands Dylan and his goons with nothing to do. Well, shit. I don't want to give them something to do. He's definitely still pissed about the paper football, and he's also likely stressed from being trapped underground for the whole school day. How close is he to my car?

He's one row away, with my driver's side door facing him.

In middle school, my friends and I had PE with him and his goons. We were the only ones who could compete against them. We used our diver's skills to combat their strength. He hated us and actively targeted me outside of PE, sometimes shoving me just to show how strong he was. I've always been too afraid to stand up to him. He torments everyone in his path, getting off on other people's misery. Now he's been pent-up for hours, so I can't afford to let him see me alone within his reach.

I have nowhere else to go, but he hasn't seen me yet. I have two options. I can run as fast as I can to my car, but he will definitely see me and that could cut it a little too close. Sneaking will be the safer option.

The parking lot is still crowded with student drivers lining up to leave. I wait for a minivan to pass, blocking their line of sight. I keep low, almost crawling behind the parked cars. Some of the other students see me and giggle to themselves. All that matters is that the goons don't see me. I circle around to my car so close I can hear them talking.

Dylan speaks with such confidence, "This is it. We are going to war."

His crew let out war cries and beat their chests.

"I'm going to join the marines where the real fighting will be."

His crew chants, "Oorah!" in unison.

One yells, "I'm going to kill a hundred of them fags!"

Another one says, "That's weak. I'm going to kill *two* hundred!"

It devolves into an incomprehensible mess of numbers

and the medals they will earn as I enter my car through the passenger's side to avoid detection. It's an awkward maneuver into the driver's seat, but I get there. They're so infatuated with their talk of glory, no one sees me drive away. They really want to fight, while I just went to great lengths to avoid conflict. Should I have just confronted them? If I had, I would have gotten my ass kicked and gotten suspended because of the school district's zero tolerance fighting policy. Both sides get in trouble no matter what the circumstances are.

CHAPTER 2

TRAFFIC IS AN ABSOLUTE NIGHTMARE on the way home. Everyone is driving to the nearest grocery store to stock up on supplies. Maybe the radio has some insight on what's going on. Everyone is giving different perspectives. One newscaster blames this predicament on President Obama's failure to negotiate with foreign leaders. Another station praises the president for his swift action to aid Hawaii. I just want to know what the hell happened. It seems like no one is sure where the missile came from and there are speculations of a second missile, but no one knows where it went. NPR says the president will address the nation today at five. It's a quarter till four, which means we have about another hour of speculation.

The second I open the door, Mom comes out and hugs me. "How was school?" Her grip is as strong as iron.

"It was really boring just sitting on the ground for hours. Caused everyone to miss most of the finals."

She lets go of me. "What will that do to everyone's GPA?"

"I think I heard the principal say something about giving everyone a passing grade."

The TV is already on, and Dad is already in his big chair. Mom sits on the couch. I sit on the floor. I've always found the carpet more comfortable because I can stretch out my legs.

President Obama stands before the podium and everything falls away. His voice is deep and concise. "My fellow Americans. Today is a day that will live in infamy. Early this morning, the rogue nation of North Korea fired a nuclear warhead at the main island of Hawaii." He pauses for a moment, letting that information sink in. "We are doing everything in our power to aid the survivors and evacuate the island. This act of aggression will not go unpunished. I ask my fellow Americans to stand together. We need to show that we won't be intimidated. We will answer this attack with justice. Not with the nuclear option. We are better than that. We are the leaders of the free world, and we will not be the reason the world ends. Our hearts, our thoughts, and our prayers go out to the families and loved ones affected by this tragedy."

Well, that was inspiring, but what about the rumor of the second missile? Does justice mean war? He didn't really give details on what happens next.

The next several days are a blur of nationalism, patriotism, and fear. The military recruitment stations have lines out the door. War has not been officially declared, but it's coming any day now. I have a few months till I turn eighteen. I don't know if I want to fight, but I'm afraid I might not have a choice.

There is no school as winter break begins. However, the

Christmas spirit is lacking as people raid grocery stores for supplies. TV isn't even an escape from the madness as every station constantly updates us on the global situation.

About a week after the bombing, China declares war on both the US and Russia. That feels out of nowhere. North Korea started this mess. Why would China want to fight both Russia and us?

As it turns out, the second missile passed through Russian air space and their automatic defenses kicked in. Bombed North Korea back to the stone age. China declared war on Russia in the name of their fallen ally. North Korea had been close allies for decades, ever sense the Korean War in the 1950s. The fact that Russia was unapologetic for the retaliation only pissed off China even more, and things very quickly escalated into large scale battles between the two nations. At the same time, the US decided to point its anger at China for letting the tragedy of Hawaii happen. The world erupted into a global conflict. The official date for the third world war is the twentieth of December 2012. I guess the Mayans were right.

I am feeling pressured by the adults in my life. The media keeps saying it is the duty of every American to defend their country. Friends who already graduated are posting on social media that they joined the military. It gets worse on Christmas when my uncle on my dad's side asks if I am going to join the fight. I tell him I'm not sure. Which isn't a lie. I'm not even done with high school yet and haven't decided on my future. My older brother Pete is in law school and has a future planned out. Ann is leaning toward the medical profession. I don't know what I'm going to do with my life. My uncle criticizes me for being an "unpatriotic coward who has no business calling himself an American."

"What am I supposed to do? I'm not done with high school yet."

Uncle Steve says, "Both my kids left school for the war effort."

"But weren't they both college dropouts? I'm not even eighteen yet."

My mother, unable to take anymore of her brother-in-law's shit, yells, "Shut up, Steve! I'm not letting my baby anywhere near this war. And if you're going to bring that kind of talk into my household, you are no longer welcome."

The argument intensifies into incomprehensible curses that end with Uncle Steve slamming the door on the way out.

Mom reopens the door, yelling, "You dodged the draft! You have no right forcing anyone else to go!" Then she slams the door again.

It won't be Christmas without a family dispute, but it's never been because of me before. It is usually because of politics though.

My mother doesn't want me anywhere near the military. Her father fought in the infantry during World War II and the Korean War. She never told me much about him, but the few stories she shared were not great. He was an abusive alcoholic and not much of a parent. Probably because of his time in combat. She spent most of her time at her friends' houses to avoid going home after school. She's afraid the military will turn me into him. My grandmother never talked about him either. If I asked, she would just take a long drag from a cigarette and stare off into space. Mom had an older brother I never met as well. He died in Vietnam. He was the one she looked up to. He would protect her from their father. When he died, she was devastated. She sees the military as something that broke her father and killed her brother. I don't blame her for encouraging me not to fight, but it's still an option. They would pay for college. I'm definitely not getting any academic or sports scholarships. I do feel the patriotic need to fight and protect my country, but I've never been much of a fighter. I am a really good shot though. Dad took me out shooting a few times when I was younger, with Uncle Steve. However, shooting a target is a lot different than shooting a living person. I don't know if I could kill. Does that make me less of a man?

After Christmas, Rick, Zack, Alex, and I decide to hang out and play some video games. We want to do an all-nighter of gaming before the end of winter break. The best place is Rick's house. He has the largest collection of gaming systems. We decide to work our way up from classic to modern games. Zack wins the majority of the older games. The more modern games are more of an all-out battle for victory. Zack isn't that good at modern first person shooters, but he puts up the best fight he can. At about three in the morning, we call it quits with a tie between Rick and I. Rick goes to his bed, and we fall asleep on whatever furniture we can find. Alex ends up on the floor because none of the furniture fits him.

It is silent for a bit, then Zack asks in a quiet voice, "Are you guys awake?"

Alex answers, "Yeah."

I say, "Not really."

Zack whispers, "I've been thinking a lot lately."

Alex answers, "About what?"

"About life. The third World War is happening, and I don't want to stay here and not do anything, but I don't want to be on the front lines."

I don't want to say anything, but Alex does. "I hear you. This whole thing is our generation's call to greatness. I want to do something too, and let's be honest, I'm a big target. I won't last long on the front lines."

Zack says, "No kidding. Doubt they would have to even aim to hit you."

They chuckle a bit.

I just roll over. I don't want to talk about the war.

Zack continues, "I'm already eighteen. I can make my own decisions. I'm joining the navy after high school. I can do my part and not have to fight on the front lines. Then after four years, I can go to college without any loans."

Alex says, "Well, if that's what you're doing, so will I. Someone has to watch after you."

Zack jokes, "A tall guy like you on a compact boat. Might get uncomfortable."

Alex says, "I'll be fine. Besides, it'll only be a matter of time before I'm running the ship. Then I get the largest bed on the boat."

Zack says, "Not if I get promoted first."

I never say a word. I couldn't join the navy. I get seasick way too easily. I went on a fishing boat in California with my dad and Uncle Steve when I was thirteen. It was my uncle's idea. My dad didn't want to go because he has trouble with seasickness, but I pestered and begged until he gave in. Dad took some medicine beforehand, to combat the seasickness and recommended I take some as well, but I thought I was tough and could handle the waves of the ocean. After about thirty minutes of being on the water, I started feeling queasy. I ended up puking over the side until I had nothing left in my stomach, then spent the rest of the time hugging the side of the ship, wishing the trip would end. My uncle and my cousins made fun of me, but Dad said the same thing happened to him the first time he was on a boat.

Then before I can appreciate the vacation, school starts again. I think there is a need to maintain normalcy in times like these. So here we are back in class, trying to pretend the world isn't literally on fire or at least blowing up.

Rather than teaching, my history teacher gives an hour long speech about patriotism and the duty of young Americans. Most of the faculty expresses their patriotism, except for Mrs. Fowler. When a couple of students talk about enlisting, she says, "I know most of you want to fight. And I understand. I really do. This is something bigger than any of us. We were attacked unjustly, and many of our fellow countrymen are gone. Just remember, the nation that fired the missiles are gone. Don't be too quick to take a life. Not when everyone is just trying to do what they think is right. You are all so young, with your whole lives ahead of you. If you want to enlist, go for it, but don't make a decision too quickly. Look at other options. Go to college first and enlist as an officer. Maybe the war will be over before you have to fight. Just slow down and think about your futures." She has never been this calm before. It feels like she's scared for us as she knows the consequences of what lies ahead.

I turn eighteen at the end of February and life starts moving faster. School continues, as always. The war is on the other side of the world, in Mongolia, Kazakhstan, and all throughout the Middle East. The pressure starts getting worse around me. All around me people are signing up for the armed forces. At the same time, the local marine base is on a constant high alert. I don't have the grades for an academic scholarship and I'm not good enough at track and field to get a sports scholarship, so I apply to Arizona Western Community College here in Yuma.

One day after school when I am doing homework, Mom comes in, "Jason, do you remember that friend of yours, Tommy?"

Tommy? Who the hell is Tommy? Wait… "Tommy, that kid who always followed me and my friends around. I wouldn't call him my friend. He was more a friend of Zack's, but only because their moms were friends."

"Well, apparently he went to the army recruiter and was deemed unfit for service due to his weight."

I laugh a bit at that.

"So you could gain an extra hundred pounds and not have to worry about the war."

I stop laughing. My mom is encouraging me to gain weight to avoid the war?

Then Dad comes in. "Jason, don't forget to register for the draft."

Mom gives him a dirty look.

"What? It's the law."

"Well, it's a dumb law." She storms off.

Dad's just trying to be helpful, but Mom is getting more protective as I get closer to finishing school. I'm going to have to make a choice soon.

Soon the government starts pushing a bill to bring back the draft. The protests are small and short lived. Most public opinion is *for* the draft. An angry old guy on the news says, "The draft is necessary because it is the only way Millennials will contribute. The war is their only chance for greatness." So much of the news is about how very little my generation has done or is useful for. Of course, we haven't done much. Most of my generation is barely out of high school. What I don't understand is how can a generation that fought so hard against the draft during Vietnam be so willing to send others to war. I suppose it's because the nation was attacked and everyone is scared, but every time I pass by the military recruitment office, there's a line out the door. It doesn't feel like there is a shortage of enlistments.

In early March, the US Military comes and has the entire senior class take the ASVAB (Armed Services Vocational Aptitude Battery) test. I remember last year, anyone could volunteer to take it, but this year it is mandatory. Not a good sign for my future. Rick ends up getting in the top percent by scoring a ninety-five. Alex and Zack both score in the seventies. I score a thirty-one, which is exactly enough for front line infantry. I get a bad feeling in my gut after finding out. Would be gentler if they just punch a sticker on me that said Front Lines. I kept second guessing my answers and not fully erasing my prior answers, which probably factored in.

My high school graduation feels weird. There are so many excited to be leaving to do their part in the war. I look around at my class, knowing most of them won't be coming back.

CHAPTER 3

SUMMER VACATION. I SPEND THE first week catching up on sleep, playing video games, and hanging out with friends. I'll decide on my future after a week or two of relaxation. For seven great days of summer vacation, I ignore the world. Mom does pester me to do chores though. I clean and dust what I'm told to. While bringing in the trash, I grab the mail. We have a *MAD* magazine for Dad, *Home and Garden* for Mom, a couple of bills, and one letter for me. It's from the US government. I don't need to open it. I already know what it says. My stomach drops as the reality I was trying to avoid hits me like a dump truck.

I have been drafted. One of the first, apparently, judging by my draft number. No more indecisiveness. The United States Government has made the decision for me.

I sit at the kitchen counter just staring at the letter.

Selective Service System

Order to Report for Induction

How am I going to tell Mom?

Dad comes into the kitchen while I am distracted. "Whatcha reading, bud?"

I don't answer, just hand the letter to him.

"Oh, no…Jason." He grabs me and holds me tight.

My body is numb. The war won't be a world away anymore.

"You were going to hang out with your friends today, right?"

My voice is almost a whisper. "Yeah. We're meeting at the park."

Dad says, "Take the car. I'll tell your mom."

"Shouldn't I tell her?"

His voice is calm. "No, I'll tell her. It will be easier to keep her calm if I tell her without you here."

Mom won't be back from her book club for another hour. I grab the keys as I leave, glancing back at dad looking at the letter with the same vacant eyes I had.

I get to the park way before we planned to meet and just sit in the car with the air conditioning on. It's too damn hot out. Why did we want to meet here? Why meet at a mostly concrete park during an Arizona summer? Bunch of fucking idiots. Let's listen to some music. All the music stations are playing commercials at the same time. Typical.

Fine, I change it to the news station. "The US is losing ground in Japan and Turkey to Chinese forces. Russia is unable to move forward in Europe. The entire European Union is holding together, refusing to let another world war destroy the continent. We go now live to our reporter in the field, Josh Brody, live in Lithuania. Josh, what is happening?"

His connection is weak. "I'm a few miles from the frontlines, and Russian forces continue to bomb the area."

Explosions echo, breaking up his signal.

"I'm with General Kareiva of the Lithuanian armed forces. General, what's your plan?"

His accent is thick, but his words are decisive. "We will not lose any more ground to the Russians. My men and my people refuse to be slaves of the Soviet Union ever again. We will fight to the last man."

I shut off my car. I don't want to hear anymore. I need to clear my head. The park is hot, but it brings a feeling of nostalgia. I have many fun memories playing in the jungle gym as a kid with my older siblings. Playing soccer with Rick and Zack in sixth grade, though we lost every game. I remember one game in particular when Zack broke his finger. Rick got a bloody nose once when the ball hit him in the face. I got kicked in the ribs with cleats and still have a small scar. That was a rough game, but it's kind of funny looking back on it. We had to play a team a year older than us, and they kicked the crap out of us. It was just a game, but they were so intense.

I'm so distracted by my memories that I don't notice Rick sneaking up behind me. "Boo!"

I jump back. "What the fuck!"

He laughs as I try to compose myself. "What are you staring at?"

"Apparently a friend with no concept of personal space." I look back at the empty field. "Remember that soccer game when we were kids and we got beat up by those older kids."

He looks at the soccer field. "Yeah, Zack's finger is still crooked. Good times, right?"

We stand in silence, staring at the field.

"Rick, I've been drafted." Wow, I didn't mean to blurt that out.

His eyes open with shock for a moment, but he quickly composes himself. "So, what are you going to do?"

"What *can* I do? I can't go to Canada. They're fighting in the war with us. And I don't speak Spanish, so Mexico isn't an option. I can't run and hide." I didn't get into a university like you did, but I don't say that part out loud. The silence continues. I don't know what else to say.

In a calm voice, Rick says, "Why don't I join you?"

"Rick, I can't ask you to throw away your life for me."

Rick says, "You didn't, but you're my best friend and I'm not going to let you go alone. I'm eighteen. I can enlist if I want to and no one can legally stop me."

"But you're signed up to go to a university on an academic scholarship."

He says, "Yeah, well, it wasn't going to cover as much as you think. And with tuition going up every year, it would cover less and less. The military will pay for everything."

"You're a good friend."

"Damn right. Besides, you need someone with real brains to keep you alive. Remember that time your brother took us to a high school party when we were in seventh grade?"

I say, "Eighth grade," as if that makes much of a difference.

Rick continues, "Not the point. When the cops came to break up the party."

I remember all too well.

"Your brother ditched us as we fled through the wash behind the house. You ran into a barbed wire fence."

I still have a scar on my stomach.

"I was the one who knew the way home in the dark and

how to treat your wound with hydrogen peroxide and close it with over the skin stitches."

I have to agree and say, "I would not have survived that night without you."

He says, "Damn right!"

I remember when I got home that night at like three in the morning, Pete was asleep on the couch. I woke him up by throwing my blood soaked shirt at him. We never got caught, but Ann was in charge of watching us when Mom and Dad went out of town from then on.

A few minutes later, Zack and Alex arrive and tell us all about the navy's requirements. They're shipping out next week. It feels too soon. Zack tells us that Dylan failed his drug test. Apparently, he tested positive for steroids. We joke about the irony and how we knew it all along. "How did you find out?"

Zack says, "My mom told me. She works with his mom." His mom really knows all the gossip around town.

I take a bit of pride in the fact that I'm a better soldier candidate than the big bad jock. But he chose to join, while I have to be forced.

We all decide to go see a cheap movie. Is this really how we're going to spend our last bit of time together? A dumb movie, then loitering in the parking lot afterward. We do this so often, but what else is there to do? There's just desert and rocks. We end up hanging outside the theater and talking longer than the movie was.

Hours later, I get home. Mom and Dad are both waiting for me at the dinner table. The silence is deafening. I don't want to sit down, but I do.

Dad breaks the silence first. "How are your friends?"

I say, "They're good. Zack and Alex ship out next week."

"That's soon. Are they ready for sea sickness?"

"I don't think they get seasick."

Dad smiles with a chuckle in his voice. "Or they haven't found out yet."

Mom blurts out, "You're moving to Canada!"

I knew she was going to push me to leave. "*Mom*, I can't hide from this."

"Yes, you can. You don't have to fight. Your brother Pete is avoiding it by going to law school."

"I think I do. I can't hide in another country. This is a world war. Canada's fighting too. And I didn't get the academic scholarships Pete got. That's why we were considering community college, but that won't keep me out of this."

Mom pleads, "Say you're a conscientious objector. Then you won't have to fight."

Dad chimes in, "If he does, then he could go to prison. And I doubt Steve will represent someone he views as unpatriotic even if it is his nephew, and we can't afford a real lawyer."

"Mom, Rick is going to join me. I can't let my best friend go to war alone. I know you're worried about me, but I have to do this."

Mom walks over and grabs me, pulling me in for a tight hug. "I'm your mother. It's my job to worry about you. I've watched you grow into a strong young man. I've seen what war does to strong young men. It breaks them. I never wanted that for you."

She doesn't let go for a long time. She knows when she does, I won't be her little boy anymore.

CHAPTER 4

AFTER RICK SIGNED UP, WE both took a medical examination with a bunch of other applicants. Rick gets called before me. I forgot my phone and all the magazines are from five years ago, so I scan the room, looking at the other future soldiers. By the looks of it, I would say a lot of them are from poor neighborhoods. Old clothes that need to be washed. There's a large white dude with a mullet. I can't tell if he has a farmer's tan or if that's just dirt.

A scrappy Hispanic dude with a pencil thin mustache sits next to me. "Hi, I'm Angel." He puts his hand out.

"Jason," and I shake his hand.

Angel looks around like he's being watched, then asks, "Are you a draftee or joining on your own?"

This feels like a loaded question, but I answer honestly, "I was drafted."

He perks up at that. "Good, that means you're one of us."

"What?"

He leans in close to whisper.

I just met you, dude. This is getting kind of weird.

"The government is clearing out the lower levels of society. I've been asking around. Got to find out who's on our side. Turns out most of the draftees have some kind of criminal record or had low test scores. That's why the ASVAB was mandatory and before the draft. We are the ones viewed by society as low value. That's the dark truth behind the draft."

Is that why I had such a high draft number? Don't let this random dude freak you out. Come on, man.

He says, "They did this back in Vietnam and they're doing it again."

That can't be true, right? "I thought this was because our nation needed us."

He smiles with crooked teeth. "They do, but they need us to not be around anymore."

Alright, smart guy. "So then why did they choose you?"

He looks around again.

Seriously, dude, no one is looking over here.

"Well, I was asked. The judge said I could either go back to prison or enlist in the army, and if I enlisted, all my past offenses would be forgiven. So, I took the deal."

Oh, so you're a paranoid criminal. "What were you being charged with?"

"Theft, and I had weed on me, so I also got charged with intent to sell, which was bullshit. I barely had a gram."

They call my name, and I spring up. "Nice meeting you." I walk away fast.

After a very intrusive medical exam where they take my blood and test every one of my senses, I'll have to come back in a few days to pick up an envelope of all my information for basic training. There are a lot more steps to getting drafted than I expected. Television makes it seem like you get drafted, then they drag you off to boot camp.

I am told to be at Camp Navajo Army Base just outside of Flagstaff, Arizona in two weeks. A bus will be available for the trip. Normally, Camp Navajo is used to train the National Guard, but due to the demand for infantry soldiers, it has been converted. I have two weeks to prepare, which feels like no time at all. I spend most of that time with my parents, at home. I pack a duffel bag of clothing and a few other essentials. Dad tries to get me to pack extra toilet paper, but I don't want to get caught with contraband. I tell him I'll take it after boot camp. Other than that, there isn't much to do. My older siblings are too busy with their college lives. My cousins are already overseas. I avoid talking to my aunts and uncles, especially after what happened during Christmas. All my grandparents died before I got to high school. So, all I can do is wait. I do exercise, but I doubt two weeks of exercise will really prepare me for the ten weeks of military training that's about to hit me.

My friends and I decide to go for one last hike a few days before Zack and Alex leave. Rick and I still have a week left. We hike to the top of one of the mountain ridges that overlooks our entire city. At the top, we sit in silence breathing hard. We've done the hike a bunch of times in high school, but it's a steep climb.

Rick catches his breath first. "Guys, this could be the last time we see this view."

I know we were all thinking it, but I was too afraid to admit it.

Zack says, "Let's make it a memorable one." He pulls

out a plastic water bottle with the words "Snake Bite" written on the side.

I lean in, trying to make out the kind of liquid. "What is it?"

"It's a special mix of chemicals important for cleaning wounds, starting fire, and…" He smiles a devilish smile. "…creating entertainment."

No way! "You brought alcohol? We can't drink that right before basic."

Zack says, "Cool your tits. You've already passed your drug test. Plus, we're only having a sip. It won't be enough to get you drunk. Besides, this is the last time we're going to all be together before we turn twenty-one." His voice fades to a more serious tone. "I want my first drink of alcohol to be with my best friends."

I've never seen this side of Zack before. He's always been loud and funny. He pours each of us a small plastic shot cup full of this so called Snake Bite.

Alex takes his cup, lifts it into the air, and declares, "To friendship!"

Rick takes his, declaring, "To adventure!"

Then I take mine. "To a brave new world!"

Zack lifts his and says, "To my best friends, may we all return home victorious and in one piece."

We drink at the same time. The alcohol burns my throat all the way down to my stomach. We all cough heavily. God, that's nasty.

Rick speaks with almost no air in his lungs, trying not to cough, "How do people drink that normally?"

My voice is hoarse. "I have no idea." I take a big gulp of water to clear the taste.

When the day finally comes, my parents and brother and sister drop me off at the bus station. Mom holds me tight. "Be safe, I need you to come home in one piece."

"I will, Mom."

Pete has dark shadows under his eyes, but he slaps me on the back and says, "Don't be stupid, but give 'em hell, little dude."

Ann pulls me in for a tight hug. "I'm going to miss you, little brother." She releases me by pushing me a little too hard, and I have to catch my balance.

Dad has tears in his eyes. I haven't seen him with tears in his eyes since his dad died two years ago. "I love you, son." His strong arms wrap around me. "I'm so proud of you."

"I love you too, Dad."

Our goodbyes come to an end. As I step onto the bus, I look back. Rick's right behind me, and our families are waving goodbye.

He smiles. "So the adventure begins."

We file into our seats. I take the window and watch as my hometown passes by my window. Stores I've never been in but driven past a hundred times. My crappy middle school. Fuck that place. A high school where we lost a track meet. A restaurant I liked going to as a kid. So many memories of home. Until we enter the freeway and leave those memories far behind.

CHAPTER 5

THE BUS FALLS QUIET AS we pass through the gates of Camp Navajo. As soon as the bus stops, a drill sergeant marches on and addresses everyone. He's a bit shorter than me, but his presence looms over us. He's extremely buff, so much so that his uniform barely contains his muscles. In a strong voice he says, "I am Drill Sergeant Burns. From here on out, you will respond with either yes or no, drill sergeant. Is that understood?"

Collectively we reply, "Yes, Drill Sergeant."

"Good, when you leave this bus, line up males on the right, females on the left. Have your luggage in your right hand and your envelope in your left. You have two minutes. Move."

The envelope has all my important paperwork, high school diploma, draft statement, and a bunch of other stuff. We awkwardly exit the bus and line up appropriately.

"Everyone, stick your left arm out. You should not be touching the person in front of you."

We have to readjust our lines.

"I want all of you to put your packet on your luggage in front of you. Then turn and face me."

Some fumble, but we all turn and face Drill Sergeant Burns.

"Now, all of you have already failed your first task. I gave you two minutes to exit the bus. Because not all of you moved with a purpose, you failed this very simple task. Now drop into the pushup position."

We drop.

"From here on out, when you are told to move, you will move with a purpose. We make things very simple for you. All commands that are given are a simple yes or no. You do not need to think. You only need to do what we say. Now start doing pushups."

We start doing push-ups.

"We will tell you everything you need to know. We will tell you the who, the where, and the when."

Some people start to struggle with the pushups.

"Now stand up and follow me and the other drill instructors into the classroom."

We do so. I want to say something clever to Rick as we go, but my eyes meet a drill sergeant's glare and the intensity in his eyes makes me bite my tongue.

In the classroom, we go over all our paperwork. Few questions are asked. Everyone is afraid of saying something stupid. We are then given a small meal wrapped in plastic. It contains a juice box, fruit snacks, a granola bar, and sunflower seeds. As we eat, we watch a video describing our future lives in the United States Army. Basically, do what you're told for the next ten weeks and you will be fine.

We get measured for clothes and are issued our military attire. Boot, shirts, pants, even underwear.

Someone asks, "Why does it matter what underwear we have?"

The overworked clothing measurer says, "You can wear whatever kind of underwear you want after basic training. Until then, this is what you get."

I get the feeling he's been asked that a lot.

The next day, they buzz off all our hair, even those of us who already had short hair. It's so everyone starts at the same point. To take away our individuality. I watch an old barber as he buzzes off Rick's blond afro. I've never seen him without it, and he looks odd. The same barber buzzes my short brown hair to almost nothing.

I ask, "So how long have you been working here?"

His voice is almost cheery. "A long time. Ten years past retirement."

"Got any advice for a new kid fresh from the draft?"

He takes a moment to think. "Hmmmm. Do what you're told and be smart. I was here the last time there was a draft. This is a hard path the world puts you on. Don't do anything stupid." He finishes my hair right as he finishes talking. "Alright, next."

Processing takes another week. There is a lot of paperwork, as well as a bunch of immunization shots. We will be living in close quarters for the next ten weeks. I bet the flu would spread like wildfire here. One of the benefits to being in the military is being able to have minor surgeries done free of charge. Rick and several other recruits get their wisdom teeth removed. They all look like chipmunks for the remaining time.

The first official day we stand outside in our brand new uniforms, the giant recruit next to me whispers, "Here comes the shark attack."

I don't have time to ask as suddenly drill sergeants line us up by yelling full volume at everything we do. No one is safe.

A slight slouch. "Stand up straight!"

A bag not lifted high enough. "Get that bag higher, recruit!"

Each one of them takes time to yell at Angel for not shaving his pencil thin mustache. "That mustache exceeds beyond your lip! Shave that thing before I do it for you!"

Our first official day begins. All the other drill sergeants fall silent and line up facing us. A short man walks past them. He's a good head shorter than all the other drill sergeants, but his voice is powerful, carrying without the need of a megaphone.

"Recruits, I am Drill Sergeant Jones. This is the first boot camp in thirty-seven years to have both draftees and volunteers. That is because our nation is at war. This is a *world* war, and our country has called upon its people to defend it. Do you understand?"

In unison, "Yes, Drill Sergeant."

"Good! You will be embarking on a strenuous path for the next nine weeks. You will be tired. You will be hungry. And you will be pushed to your limit. But you can and will overcome it. The fastest way out is by completing basic training. Now look to your left. Now look to your right. Those are your battle buddies. You will depend on them to succeed. If one of you fails, *all* of you fail. Stand together and you will complete your training. Understand?"

In unison, "Yes, Drill Sergeant."

There are no easy days in boot camp. We run every day, and we run everywhere. If one person fails, we all fail. We all pay for it, and no one fails more than Melvin. He's so out of shape, I doubt he's seen his feet in years. Dude can't even walk in a straight line. His timing is so bad he keeps bumping into the people in front of him. He can't even stand still. When we hold attention, he always has to scratch something when Drill Sergeant Burns is walking by, forcing everyone to pay for his mistakes with more work. He should just be quiet and make all our lives easier. The demand for soldiers is so high that they won't boot him, causing us to run more than any other company.

Every time we run, Drill Sergeant Burns sings cadence. His favorite cadence is "Mama Mama."

> Mama mama, can't you see,
> what the army's done to me.
>
> They put me in a barber's chair,
> spun me around I had no hair.
>
> Mama mama can't you see,
> what the army's done to me.
>
> They took away my favorite jeans,
> now I'm wearing army greens.
>
> Mama mama can't you see,
> what the army's done to me.

I use to date beauty queens,
now I love my M16.

Mama mama can't you see,
what the army's done to me.

I use to drive a Cadillac,
now I carry one on my back.

The lyrics are burned into our collective minds. I've never been this exhausted in my life. We never get enough sleep. I've been catching myself thinking in the past tense. Why? Who am I talking to besides me? I need rest, but nope, we've got to run even more.

One morning we are woken up extra early and line up in front of our bunks out of instinct. I have to fight to keep my eyes open. I hear rain on the thin roof. This is going to be another bad day.

Lightning cracks as Dill Sergeant Burns Marches past me in a full rain gear. "Ruck march!"

Melvin says, "Running in the rain would be bad for our health."

I want to tell him to shut up, but I could get dragged into it too.

Drill Sergeant Burns stops his march and smiles at Melvin. "You're right, Meatball."

Shocked, Melvin says, "Really? Wait, my name is Melv—"

For a fraction of a second, he looked happy until Drill Sergeant Burns cuts him off. "You are now Meatball because you are round like a ball and nothing but meat!" Drill Sergeant Burns shoves a mop and bucket into Meatball's hands. "Now! Go mop up the rain! For the sake of your fellow recruits!"

Meatball stumbles for words, but Drill Sergeant Burns chases him out. "Move!"

"Now, does anyone else want to help mop up the rain?"

No one speaks, standing motionless and hoping the lack of movement will prevent the predator from striking.

"Suit up!"

We got ready in record time.

Hours later, we return soaking wet. Every ounce of me is soaked, especially my socks. Each step feels like walking in a puddle. I just want to take a mildly warm shower and pass the fuck out. Then in comes Meatball with a bucket full of rainwater, looking defeated.

Angel asks, "Did you get all the rain?"

Meatball turns and looks out the window, his gaze staring off for miles. "No, but Burns told me I could stop." With dead eyes, he looks for dry clothes.

Rick and I get to be bunkmates. As we clean up, he whispers, "I think I heard Burns say something about a gas chamber tomorrow."

"That can't be good."

"Oh, but it is!" says the smiling face of Hercules, a goliath of a man occupying the bunk next to us. A true demigod among us. My skull is the size of his biceps. He plans to go into Special Forces after basic training. I have no doubt he will succeed. "The gas chamber is when they lock us in a room and douse us with tear gas."

I ask, "Why are you excited about that?"

Hercules says, "My older brother did it and the gas

cleared out his sinuses so much that he no longer has allergies."

Rick calls, "Bullshit."

Smiling with excitement, Hercules says, "Just wait. Tomorrow you'll see for yourself."

I say to Rick, "Are you still happy you joined?"

He punches my arm. "Hell no, but I ain't going nowhere now. Five bucks says I can last longer in the chamber than you."

"You're on." We shake on it. I could always hold my breath for a long time. That's how I'll win.

The best part of this whole experience has to be chow time. I was expecting mush soup, but sweet damn, I was wrong. There's fresh spaghetti with the best meatballs I've ever had. The sirloin steak has to be fresh from the cow. There is no other way it could taste this good. Chow time is the only part of this ordeal everyone collectively looks forward to.

The worst part, on the other hand, for me at least, is the bathrooms. I'm a man who likes his privacy in the restroom, but that is long gone. There are no stalls with two parallel rows of toilets facing each other like in high school. To add more stress to an open bathroom, there's also a time limit. When a drill sergeant first gave me ten seconds to take a shit and wipe, that was the most stressful dump I had ever taken.

We have been briefed extensively on the proper use of gas masks, but they go over all of it again. Then we grab each other's shoulders and march into the chamber. They release the gas. We are told that if any of our snot ends up on the floor, we will be sent back in to clean it up. We do a quick workout of jumping jacks to get us breathing hard.

Then Drill Sergeant Burns instructs, "Remove your masks."

Immediately, everyone starts coughing. I can't hold my breath very long after a workout. My eyes burn. I feel my lungs catch on fire. Snot pours out my nose, and I catch it and wipe it on my uniform. I refuse to come back in here. My skin feels wrong. For the love of God, make it stop. I can't take it anymore. The snot gushes like Niagara Falls, but I won't let any of it hit the floor. My eyes feel like they're bleeding. Please make it stop.

It feels like forever until the drill sergeants let us leave. We have to flap our arms to get any remaining chemicals off our uniforms and look like a bunch of coughing birds. Several people fall and are immediately picked up by the person behind them. I see several people puke. I feel as though I could too, but I hold it back as best I can. Neither of us win the bet.

There is no rest, ever. Sleep is the most sacred resource. At least I don't have to think as much. Drill Sergeant Burns tells me all I need to know. Run, jump, go over there, do as you're told. When someone fucks up something simple, drop into the push-up position. When someone says something to undermine Drill Sergeant Burns's authority, we do more push-ups. That's taking a little too long to stop. Sometimes it is one of Angel's buddies from juvy. Usually this guy Luis, and it's almost a shame when he stops. He is really funny, but Drill Sergeant Burns doesn't like funny. Luis boasted that he ended up in juvy for theft, vandalism, and grand theft auto. Stole one car for a joy ride and got all those charges.

CHAPTER 6

DRILL SERGEANT BURNS BECOMES MORE of a teacher during combat training and doesn't yell as much. We learn about our equipment as well as what the Chinese and Russians use. We practice shooting and running combat drills and learn proper breaching of buildings. We learn how to move as a unit, to depend on the person behind you and support the person in front. All of this is done in full gear. We use blanks to simulate the weight, as well as real rifles but with pugs on the front just in case a live round ends up in the gun. We learn proper cleaning and care for our rifle, our lifeline. Then we learn close combat techniques.

"The first rule of combat is there are no rules in combat. Do not try to fight fair because your enemy won't. They will do whatever it takes to kill you. You will have to do the same. There are two types of people in a fight. There is the quick and there is the dead." Drill Sergeant Burns yells, "Who are you?"

We yell back, "Quick!"

Drill Sergeant Burns yells, "Who are they?"

We yell back, "Dead!"

We practice striking against dummies. We are not allowed to hold back on the dummies. Break limbs at the joints. Break the knee by kicking it inward. Throat strikes and groin strikes. Never fight fair.

We are trained in proper grappling techniques, how to take an opponent down quickly and effectively, and defenses. We spend a lot of time rolling with an opponent to gain practical experience. This leads to a grappling tournament as a morale boost. I feel confident. I've been a fast learner in grappling and even been able to keep up with other recruits who wrestled in high school. These past three weeks have put me in the best shape of my life. I can carry over a hundred pounds of equipment for miles. For the first time in my life, I have six pack abs. I am strong.

Our arena is a grass field surrounded by the rest of the recruits. The female recruits have their tournament first. Women weren't drafted, but a fair amount signed up to fight for their country. They grapple, and we cheer, but my mind is preoccupied with thinking of a strategy against every possible opponent. I've got this in the bag.

Drill Sergeant Burns calls me to go first for the men, then calls my opponent, Hercules.

All right, here's the plan. I go for the takedown. He's big, but I can push through that. I have enough strength to topple him. I just need to get a good grip on his right leg. Then I'll get on top and get him in an arm bar. Perfect plan.

"Begin!"

I rush forward, duck low, and reach for his right leg. Hercules sprawls, throwing his legs back and dropping all of his weight on me. He easily weighs three hundred pounds. I collapse beneath this sudden weight. I still try to reach his leg, but my grip is compromised. I feel two pythons rap around my stomach and begin to squeeze. He lifts me up and throws me to the side. My loose grip fails and I fly away, landing hard on the ground.

The crowd reacts to my landing with cheers of encouragement. "Get up!" "You can do it!"

I shake my head, trying to stay focused. Ok, I need a new plan. But Hercules grabs me again, wrapping his arms around my neck. Maybe I can slip out, but his grip is made of steel so I don't go anywhere. He squeezes, and air stops entering my lungs. I tap his arm quickly to show I'm defeated. He wins without breaking a sweat.

They cheer for the great Hercules.

I return to my spot next to Rick as Luis jumps in for the next match.

Rick says, "Not bad."

"Not bad? He wiped the floor with me."

"Remember, that's the Greek God of strength. Be happy he didn't break you in half." We watch as Hercules suplexes Luis high in the air, then slams him down with a thud, ending the match with a technical knockout. Hercules comes out the champion. No one is able to take him down.

Physical exercise becomes less prevalent as lectures and learning take priority. It feels like school. We are encouraged to learn but not to think. Follow the rules and not question, but act in the moment. Then comes more fighting.

We stab dummies with bayonets, then are given padded sticks to simulate the rifle with bayonets. So begins more practical training in the form of another tournament. Hercules beats everyone easily. He's just too powerful. Rick gets the first hit, but in a tournament based on points, he still loses to the demigod's superior strength. I'm one of the last, and I have a plan. Hercules has fought in thirty rounds so far this time, so he has to be getting tired. I can use that to my advantage. I can keep my distance and have him come to me.

As I get ready, Drill Sergeant Burn pulls me aside. "Listen."

This can't be good.

"You think too much. That's why you did bad during your grappling match. Don't think. Just attack."

"But I have a plan."

"Shut up. Everyone has a plan until they get punched in the face. Don't think. Just attack." He pushes me into the circle.

The demigod towers over me.

Don't think. Just attack. Don't think.

"Begin!"

I attack, stabbing with the tip. That's a lethal point. Hercules counters with a large hit that rocks my head, but I keep stabbing. He swings again. I duck, using my height difference to my advantage. Keep moving. Stay aggressive. For every hard swing he throws at me, I unleash a barrage of quick stabs. I can take any hard hit, thanks to the padding. I press forward, but he doesn't back down. I keep attacking. We trade blows. My headgear is getting messed up, but I keep stabbing. "Come on!" I can take anything you dish out. The round ends. Hercules is stunned. I won. I got more points, but I got bruised. Christ, he hits hard, but I toppled the champion.

As we march back to the classroom for a lecture before we can be dismissed, everyone congratulates me.

Hercules says, "You are a worthy opponent. Stay scrappy, little one."

Little one? I'm five feet ten. That's not little. It's not my fault you were blessed by the gods to be six feet ten of pure muscle. Instead, I say, "Thanks. I got plenty of bruises to remember you by."

He smiles and smacks me on the back.

Ow, there's another one.

Finally, we get to do some shooting with real guns and bullets. We get to shoot large machine guns, grenade launchers, and everything the army will issue us. It's important to be able to handle any weapon in the field. We also learn how to disassemble and properly maintain each one. I thought I was a good shot until I see some of the others shoot. A couple get offered to go to sniper school. I hit my target, just not always a bullseye. Meatball can't handle shooting the automatic rifle and loses control of it, nearly blowing his head off. Drill Sergeant Burns yells at him for a straight hour.

Then training comes to an end. Ten long, hard, grueling weeks finally end. We march for our graduation. Many of the recruit's parents come for graduation day, including my parents. We embrace as soon as the ceremony is over and the drill sergeants dismiss us. Rick's parents don't talk to me. I understand. Their golden child followed me into this, but it was his choice. I tell my parents about all the stuff I went through. Now it doesn't seem as bad. Dad gives me a roll of toilet paper, and I hide it away. Soon I'll ship out into the great unknown. Mom and Dad say they'll send care packages when they can.

I keep on a brave face even though I know this could be the last time I see my family. I can't think that way. I can't let that be true. I have to believe I'll come back. I'm stronger now. I can do anything.

We hug one last time before I have to go, and I thank them for coming.

Back in our barracks, I see Angel. He left the graduation ceremony as soon as he could and is just sitting in here reading letters. "Who are those letters from?"

Without looking up, he replies, "They're from some friends still in the joint. They want to know if taking the offer from the army is worth it."

"Would you recommend it?"

He shrugs. "So far, yes. It hasn't been too bad. Feels similar to prison. The clothing and food are better, but this is just the beginning. The clock on the enlistment hasn't really started yet. It all depends on where they send us."

That's something I haven't thought too much of. And now that training is over, I have a year of service before I can be discharged. Rick signed up for four years, because every year of service equals a year of free college. I can't just bail after my year of service and abandon him. I should stay as long as he stays.

CHAPTER 7

WE RECEIVE MORE IMMUNIZATION SHOTS before we deploy, and they make us all sick. The worst one was for anthrax, and we ended up bed ridden for a week. Angel, Luis, Rick, Meatball, and I take the longest to fully recover while everyone else is shipped off. Instead of sending us to join the rest of the unit after recovery, we get stamped as replacements for a unit somewhere in Africa. At least we get to say goodbye to Hercules when he leaves for ranger school.

Rick and I receive a bunch of letters from Zack and Alex. They both got some kind of technical job on the same aircraft carrier, the *USS Bush*. I think of how tall Alex was and him having to live in those cramped corridors. We write back about our experiences. We're given our phones back, but I doubt we'll have service on a regular basis, so letters and emails are probably our best bet to stay in contact with those we care about.

We don't know where we're going because everything is on a need to know basis. Luis bets they aren't telling us because they don't know either. It won't matter till we get there anyway, and we have a long flight ahead. We sit together in a large cargo plane with a bunch of other soldiers being sent out for other deployments, as well as various cargo. It's cramped and we have to yell over the sound of the engines.

I lie on the cold metal floor and try to sleep. I dream of my mother's brother as he first gets off the plane in Vietnam. I see my grandfather getting on a landing craft off the Normandy beachhead. I see my ancestor marching in the Tennessee countryside in his blue uniform. I see an ancestor in a kilt with a beat up sword and a wooden shield on his back, hiking down from the highlands. He looks so much like me but with long, greasy hair. He looks back at me. "Nervous about the first fight? Good."

I wake up. The sun is bright as we walk off the plane.

An officer greets us, "Welcome to Cairo, troops."

I always wanted to see Egypt, but I doubt I'll be doing a lot of sightseeing while I'm here. We report to a Major Meek to find out what we're doing. He tells us to report to a Captain Miles, who sends us to a Lieutenant Mills, who then sends us to a Sergeant McIntyre.

McIntyre looks to be in his early thirties. His buzz cut has a light red tint. I wonder how red his hair actually is. "So you guys are the replacements?"

I answer, "Yes, sir," as everyone else stays quiet.

Jerks. None of them want to say anything. Luis and Angel plan to ride out their service as easily as possible while Rick finds it funny that I will have to take the brunt of whatever crap gets thrown. Meatball is probably distracted by something. I would rather not have him with us, but we're probably stuck with him.

Sergeant McIntyre says, "Alright, you guys are in the

second Humvee. It's parked in space two. Here's a map of our route. Memorize it and return it to me in thirty minutes." He hands me a small map of the city with a highlighted route. "Drop your stuff in tent number two. Get used to that number. It will define your stay here. Gear up. We leave shortly." He sounds so casual.

I try to say, "But—"

He pushes us out.

"What are we doing here?"

Sergeant McIntyre says, "Exactly what I just told you, now *go!*"

The tent is empty except for six cots. We drop our packs on our desired beds and gear up. My eyes remain glued to the map. Maybe if I stare at it long enough, it will remain in my head. Then we rush out to our Humvee. It looks brand new. No scratches, no dents, and has shiny tan paint. All the other vehicles are covered in dents from what must have been many gun fights. Angel and Luis run off to get ammo.

A soldier from Humvee number one sees us. "So you cherries are the new number two. Sorry to say, that's a shit number deal. Last three squads to occupy that number died."

I'm too busy still staring at the map to give them any of my attention, but Rick says, "Aside from being shit, what happened to the last three squads?"

"Well, the various terrorist groups in this city like to target the second car in a convoy."

Rick asks, "Why didn't anyone else take the new Humvee?"

The soldiers look at each other and nod. "It's bad luck to ditch a vehicle that's earned its name." The soldier in the first Humvee knocks on its side and says, "Ain't that right, Pennywise."

Odd name for a Humvee. Isn't that the clown from *IT*?

Meatball says, "Wait, we're fighting terrorists?"

"Yep, several different terrorist groups backed by different foreign governments. All of them want control of Egypt. The US does our fighting ourselves."

I ask, "What's the mission?"

Sergeant McIntyre walks by and takes the map out of my hands. "Don't kill the civilians and don't die."

Rick asks, "What are the rules of engagement?"

Sergeant McIntyre says, "Only fire if fired upon." He gets into a gas tanker.

Angel and Luis get back just as we start up the Humvee. The other vehicle pulls out and lines up.

I say, "Rick, take shotgun. You're better with the radio than any of us. Angel and Meatball, you guys take the back seats. Luis, you take the fifty." We're all the same rank, but if I'm driving, I'm organizing this the way I want it.

Meatball says he wants to take the fifty. I think back to the shooting range at boot camp. He had the worst fire control out of anyone. There is no way I'm letting him have control of a fifty-caliber machine gun in a city full of civilians, so I tell him just that and everyone else agrees. He looks upset, but no one cares. We end up having to load our weapons as we go. I don't have the map fully committed to memory, but I bet I can wing it. Most of the street names are way too hard to pronounce. So, my plan is to just follow the first vehicle and not get distracted.

We take the highway, driving fast. I squeeze the wheel until my knuckles turn white. I have to stay close to the lead vehicle but not too close, all at high speed. I can hear Rick grunting and talking to himself over the sound of the engine, but I don't want to take my eyes off the lead vehicle. "You figure out what you're doing?" I ask him.

"Yeah, for the most part. The radio hasn't been set up correctly, so I'm having to do that. My main concern is this touch screen computer. It has a GPS, but everything is password protected."

Meatball speaks up from the back. "Don't mess with it. You could blow up the car."

Angel says, "All military vehicles have that to keep the enemy from any important info. I bet the self-destruct is all handled by satellites. They wouldn't let the grunts make that kind of decision. Gives us too much power."

Rick says, "Well, all it's doing is keeping us from that important info."

"When we get back to base, we can figure out the password." I pull off the freeway and enter the city.

The city is full of old architecture with modern city elements. We pass stores that would be in any city, like restaurants, barbers, clothing stores, pawnshops, and residential apartments. None bare any real marks of war until we pass a McDonalds with blown out windows and a collapsed roof. In fact, the only buildings with any damage are businesses that originated in the US.

Angel says it first. "I don't think they want the US here anymore."

Rick says, "That's because the US backed their brutal dictator for decades."

Oh boy, here comes some knowledge from Encyclopedia Rick.

"They had a revolution in 2011 to oust President Hosni Mubarak. He came to power in an election where he was the only candidate after his opponents died in 1981. He repressed his people through brutal tactics. The US backed him because he sold oil to us."

Meatball asks, "What about the pyramids? All the textbooks go on about how important the ancient Egyptians were."

Rick continues, "Well, they were, and Egypt's economy is heavily based around tourism, but it's primary export is oil to the US. My guess is that's why we're here. To protect the US oil fields."

"If they're so rich in oil, why hasn't Russia and China invaded? Why are we the only military presence here?" Angel asks.

Rick shrugs. "Maybe they're waiting. If the natives don't want us here, then all they have to do is sell weapons to the radicals, promote how great communism is, and then boom, the government topples. Eventually, the investment here will be too costly for the US to maintain its hold and we'll leave."

Meatball asks, "How do you know all this?"

I want to say it's because Rick is a genius and way too smart to be here, but instead, Rick says, "Because I followed the news when it was happening. What were you doing?"

Angel says, "He was too busy eating junk food and playing video games."

Meatball yells, "Fuck you. At least I had video games, you convict."

We hear Luis's sarcastic laugh from outside. "Ha!"

I don't look behind me, but I know Angel isn't impressed.

We reach the new oil fields just outside the city. It's a heavily guarded base with a militarized train track leading north to the Mediterranean. Three trucks leave our convoy, and three different trucks join. Sergeant McIntyre goes out and talks to someone, then gets in one of the new tankers. Then we drive back the way we came, through the city.

I ask, "Any idea what the point of that was?"

Angel says, "Oil, bro. How else is it going to get back to base? We gotta take it just to use it and come back for more."

Not very exciting. Everyone else from basic got shipped to the front. Here we are driving in a big circle.

I see a blue light in the corner of my eye and ask, "Rick, are you on your phone right now?"

Rick says, "Yeah. I'm researching news articles to learn what's happening here."

"Dude, I need you to help me navigate."

"I can do both. For example, in about twenty minutes we'll reenter the freeway and head back to base."

From up top, Luis yells, "Hey, can I drive next time? I have the most experience with high speed chases."

I yell back, "No, because of those high speed chases you never got a license."

Luis pleads, "Come on, man. I'm the best driver out of all of us."

"We'll think about it." I look at Rick and shake my head.

Angel laughs from behind me.

It takes us twenty minutes to get back to the freeway.

Meatball complains again, "That was so boring."

It was for them, but I've been stressed the whole time trying to keep up with the first car. Then from the opposite direction on the freeway, a sedan-sized car careens through the median and smashes into the first car, exploding into a large fireball full of metal debris. The sound hurts my ears, and I swerve the vehicle to avoid hitting the wreckage. Orders blast from the radio, telling us to stop and form a perimeter. I slam on the brakes. Two tons of steel cannot stop on a dime. Sparks and smoke shoot from the wheels as we screech to a stop. Still on the fifty, Luis stumbles, kicking me in the back of the head, but he holds on as we come to a complete stop. I grab my rifle and jump out of the safety of the Humvee.

The first vehicle, known as Pennywise, is completely destroyed and the fire still burns bright. They're all dead inside. There is nothing I can do for them. I stare for longer than I realize. It's the first time I've ever seen someone die, let alone a car full of people.

Sergeant McIntyre keeps barking orders to set up a perimeter and stay away from the wreckage. Luis stays on the fifty-cal. The rest of us fan out into fortified positions. Training kicks in, and I switch the safety off my M4 assault rifle. The gun can't switch to safety unless there is a round in the chamber. My eyes scan every car that passes. I don't trust any of them. They slow down to view the wreckage. I don't look at my teammates, trusting they're keeping an eye out as well.

A singular shot is fired. I turn and drop to one knee. The gunner of vehicle four collapses. A soldier points to the east, and everyone starts shooting in that direction. Thirty seconds pass, but it feels longer. We all stop and reload. Someone hops back into vehicle four and guns it back to base. Faster than calling an evac since we're not far from base. More rounds start popping off. I turn back to the burning vehicle, ready to fire. The unfired bullets have begun to discharge from the heat. I take cover in front of my Humvee until the bullets stop popping off.

We open a lane of traffic and wave cars through. Everyone keeps their guns at the ready. We wait for the base's fire department to deal with the wreckage, but by the time they got here, the fire has pretty much burned out though there is still a danger of more ammunition going off from the heat. Then we wait for a truck from base to tow what's left behind. At base, we remove the bodies from the car. I got volunteered because I'm new and for some reason, when they looked for people to help, the rest of my companions had vanished.

The smell is horrible. I almost puke, but I hold it back and try to swallow it down. The taste of military food burns my throat. I grab what I believe to be an arm and pull. It breaks off with a wet crunch. Unprepared for the momentum change, I fall. Dark liquid oozes out of the joint. I can't hold the puke back a second time. The bland meal from the day before bursts out.

Laughter erupts from all around.

A soldier says, "Hey, cherry needs a hand?"

This only makes the laughter worse.

I find the rest of the squad at the tent. "Where the hell did you guys go?"

Meatball sheepishly looks away. "Bathroom. Why is everyone calling us cherries?"

Angel answers, "We wanted to find the mess hall. We used that same term in juvy. That's what you call newbies until they pop their cherry with some kind of fight."

Rick comes in with a thick folder full of paper.

I ask, "What's that for?"

"Oh, this?" He shakes it in front of my face with a crazed look in his eyes. "This is the paperwork I have to fill out to get the password for the computer in our truck."

Meatball asks, "Why?"

Rick turns to Meatball with a twitch in his eye. "Why?" He drops the thick folder on the ground. "Because there can't be a simple solution with these people. Because I spent the last three hours in a circle, trying to find our commanding officer." Each time he says "because" he takes a step closer to Meatball. "Because I have to prove my identity. Because basic logic doesn't apply to these people. Because the only way to do that is with documentation. Why do you ask? Because bureaucracy, *that's* why!" Rick stands less than an inch from Meatball now.

Meatball backs away sheepishly and starts going through his stuff.

Rick sits down on the floor and begins going through his many papers. He spent his first night filling out paperwork, furiously mumbling to himself.

I can't sleep. I keep thinking about the burned bodies in the car and staring at my hands. I couldn't clean them off entirely and no one had gloves. They're stained black from the small remains of a human being that was alive just a few hours ago.

Explosions wake up the others and we rush out, grabbing our guns. Papers fly everywhere, but only our tent seems to care.

Sergeant McIntyre is walking by in flip-flops, casually brushing his teeth. He looks us up and down, "Don't bother, cherries. It happens every night. The spineless fucks leave active mortars in tubes full of ice. When the ice melts, the mortar fires. There's no point in getting so worked up. You'll get used to it."

Meatball asks, "Shouldn't we find cover?"

Sergeant McIntyre shrugs. "If you want, but their aim is pretty shitty."

An explosion erupts two hundred yards away, on an empty landing pad.

We drop to the ground, but McIntyre just stands there.

"See, shitty aim."

CHAPTER 8

S O LIFE CONTINUES FOR TWO weeks. The squad with the most experience gets promoted to lead. They say it's still safer than number two, but I doubt that now. We drive out daily, do a loop around the city, switch out the oil tanks at the oil fields beyond the city, and then drive back. All without access to our highly advanced computer. At one point, Rick spent the entire day on the phone talking with the manufacturer to bypass the bureaucracy because that was going nowhere. I say all day because he was on the phone literally all day—twenty-four hours straight. He had to get permission to use a landline because the cell service was kind of shit even in a modern city, something to do with China blocking and intercepting satellite signals.

Meatball never shut up about how boring it all was. He wants some real action. Angel and Luis are involved in the gambling circuit on base. They started winning all kinds of paraphernalia. Angel won a genuine samurai sword that he now sleeps with every night. The superiors don't care at all. Apparently if a weapon can be used by a civilian, then we are allowed to have it. This feels really laid back compared to the stories about the rest of the war.

"I heard in Turkey the Russians skinned everyone in a city and now use the leather as uniforms."

"No, that was the Chinese in Kazakhstan."

"Did you hear Syria is going to start using chemical weapons?"

"Why? I thought that the entire area was destroyed."

"This is their last strike to stay relevant. It will be their last stand."

All rumors that sound scary, while the real death toll is kept secret.

We have to get special clearance to go into the city because it has been deemed hostile. I've yet to see any hostility, aside from our first day. So I spend my days, after oil truck exchange, just hanging out. I tried gambling with Angel and Luis but lost all my money, so I avoid that now. I socialize with others on base. They like to keep to their prospective units unless they're gambling. So, what to do? I read and reread whatever I can find. I've read every article in a Playboy from the nineties.

However, the best pastime is the makeshift sports. There is a building that was abandoned mid-construction and we converted into a basketball court. I hop in on a game almost every day. I've become quite good at shooting hoops. We have to do PT to stay sharp as infantry too, but I'll do whatever to fight off the boredom.

If this is what my life will be like for the next year, it feels kind of like a waste. I'm not really needed here.

I am able to make calls home every so often. I never have

much to report. I can hear the relief in Mom's voice when I tell her about the tedium of my current situation.

Then one day we get issued new suits to protect us from chemical weapons. We learned how to use these back in basic, but they make us stand in rows and we go through the routine all over again. These outfits are old and dusty. My best guess is that they're leftovers from Operation Desert Storm in 1991. They don't fit well and add to the heat. Lieutenant Mills throws some tear gas at us as a test. Rick starts coughing because of a small tear in the mask. He's told to go get a new one from storage, but they're all out and he must once again go through military bureaucracy to get a new one. He almost bites through his helmet at that.

When we go out on our daily circle of the city with our new gear, Rick just put duct tape on the tear.

I ask, "They really didn't have any spares?"

Rick crushes the pencil in his hand as he fills out more paperwork. "No, all the spare masks were sent to battlefields with more strategic importance."

Meatball mutters, "There's no action here anyway."

Angel says, "Shut up, Meatball! I have good news for you, Ricky boy."

Rick perks up. "Did you win a mask in a bet?"

"Nope. Type admin123 as your username into the computer and password456, no caps."

Rick freezes for a second, then types. The screen lights up. "You have got to be fucking kidding me! How did you find that out?"

Angel says, "I just asked around on base. The question is why didn't you do that?"

Rick grits his teeth. "Because I was trying to go through the proper chain of command."

Luis calls down from the gun, "Fuck the chain of command. We make the rules."

I can't hold it in any longer. I start laughing. It was too simple, but he just couldn't see it.

"Shut the fuck up, Jason. It's not funny."

Angel and Meatball start laughing too. "Yes. Yes, it is."

It's nice having the computer work, but it's relatively unneeded. Its purpose is to help us map our route, but we just follow the lead car and it's been the same route each time. So the days continue. We do our loop and fight boredom. Rick tries to get a new mask every day but gets nowhere. He got a replacement that was ripped in a different spot. Then he got one with cracked lenses and couldn't just get new lenses, so he had to get a new mask entirely and that ended up having a puncture on the cheek. He put in another order for a new one and duct taped what he had.

Lieutenant Mills has grown tired of it and blames Rick. "How dare you damage this army's equipment! Do you know how much it costs to replace that?"

"Sir, it came this way."

"Excuses! You make a mockery of us all! Now get a new one."

"But, sir—"

"*Now*, private!" Rick actively tries to avoid Mills but never can. Must have it out for him.

CHAPTER 9

ANOTHER DAY AND WE PREP for the loop. However, today Rick wants to man the gun. He's tired of dealing with the computer. I know the loop so well I could do it blindfolded. Angel and Luis take the back seats and Meatball takes over the computer. Letting him man the computer was the only way to keep him from getting to man the fifty. None of us trust his trigger fingers.

About halfway to the oil fields, Meatball complains, "God damn it, there's no comfortable way to wear this thing." He shifts around in his chemical resistant suit. "Would it of killed them to make it just a little more baggy around the groin?"

I agree but say, "Because people are cheap and they don't care how comfortable it is as long as it's effective."

Luis says, "What do you need extra room down there for anyway?"

Meatball grunts. "My dick needs breathing room."

Luis says, "I doubt you need that much space."

Meatball threatens, "Don't make me whip it out."

Luis says, "That's a little forward. You have to buy me dinner first."

Meatball yells, "Fuck off!" and gives them the middle finger from the front seat, but Angel and Luis laugh it off.

The radio sounds off, "Incoming chemical ordinance! I repeat, incoming chemical ordinance."

Shit, shit, shit, shit!

We scramble to put on our masks and seal up our suits. We close the thick glass of our windows. My face instantly starts to sweat in the mask.

I hear Rick's muffled voice from the roof. "Holy shit."

Missiles explode above the city, showering dense yellow gas everywhere. Rick drops in and closes the hatch. The vehicle is sealed. They covered this in boot camp. Yellow gas means it's chlorine based and that shit will eat through a filter.

Over the radio, the lead car yells, "Get out of the city now!"

The convoy speeds south. The yellow clouds cut down our visibility.

I press the accelerator to the floor and the engine roars, accelerating us forward.

The radio, "Incoming ordinance on the oil fields!"

That route is out.

"Rendezvous southwest of the city!"

Gas is slowly seeping into the car.

Come on, go faster. I hear coughing. "Hold on, we're almost there." I hold my breath as we zoom past shadows. I hear a car crash behind me, but I keep going. I can't stop. The coughing gets more violent. Shit, come on, how much of this shit is there?

We burst out of the yellow cloud, into a clear view. I glance in the side mirror to see the entire city shrouded in yellow. "Holy fucking shit!"

The radio blares, "Keep moving. We need to stay upwind from the gas." I see Rick shaking in violent coughs.

No! I try to take off my mask to give to him, but Meatball smacks me, "Focus on the road!"

"Rick's mask is compromised!"

Angel yells, "I know! We'll help him. You get us out of here."

Meatball reaches back, and I hear them yelling to say calm and breathe. I hear duct tape rip. I glance back as often as I can. Through the violent coughing and shaking, Rick cries out.

I reach back with one hand and grab him. "Hold on, buddy!"

His grip is tight and gets tighter with each cough, then loosens and goes limp.

No. Please, God, no! Not like this. You can't leave me like this.

An hour later, we stop at a rally point. We were only in the gas for about ten minutes. We lay Rick down. Blood drips from the small tear on the side of his mask. The gas caused his lungs to bleed so bad that he drowned in his own blood. I take off his mask, and blood pours out, staining the sand. All the veins in his eyes have popped, robbing him of his blue eyes.

I hold the lifeless body of my best friend. My tears cloud up my mask. How do I do this without you?

Someone puts their hand on my shoulder, but I don't look. I just walk away and sit alone, staring out at the old city. Less than ten months left to go.

CHAPTER 10

WITHIN A WEEK WE'RE SENT back into the city for cleanup. Everything has a yellow tint and the ground is stained red. We pile the bodies of civilians in the street to be burned and bag up our dead to be shipped home. Major Meek and Captain Miles died from gas exposure on base. Lieutenant Mills's vehicle crashed in the gas cloud. Chlorine-based gases eat through a filter in thirty seconds. If I had gone any slower, I would have joined them.

I feel dead inside. What was the point of any of this? There was no glory, no great battle where the sacrifices meant something. All we did was drive in a circle for weeks, picking up oil to be used and refilled the next day. Neither Rick nor I ever fired our weapons. All I can do is pile up bodies in pits to be burned. It's the cheapest way of disposing of contamination, but this doesn't feel like the proper method. The dark smoke has a yellow tint to it.

The biohazard suit is even more uncomfortably hot while I stand next to a fire. No one talks to me, and I'm fine with that. I don't have anything to say. How am I going to face Rick's parents? This is all my fault. I should have given him my mask. He was the one with the bright future in front of him, not me. I don't have anything waiting back home. He could have been the next Bill Gates or the next president. Instead, he drowned in his own blood miles from home because the army didn't view us as important enough to issue undamaged gas masks.

The oil fields were bombed with radioactive material. It is unsafe to be anywhere near them. The point of the mission is gone. After a week of cleaning up, we get new orders. We aren't done with the clean up by any means. There are bodies everywhere, but all surviving troops are being sent to Turkey. The casualties are apparently astronomical, but they won't give us an exact number, leading to more rumors.

The army collected all the ammo, equipment, and non-irradiated fuel they could salvage. Corpse cleanup was never the priority. No nation claimed responsibility for the bombing, but the going rumor is that it was Syria's last strike before their total collapse.

This front is over for ground troops. All surviving military personnel are loaded onto planes. There's maybe about a hundred left from an operating base of five hundred. I look back at the dead city. "What was the point of any of this?"

Sergeant McIntyre keeps me moving. "It doesn't matter. Just keep looking forward. We are needed up north in Turkey."

Turkey is a bombed out wasteland with few trees and even fewer buildings. This has been a battleground since the beginning. The battle rages high in the sky now. Planes fly at Mach speed, shooting at targets on the edge of the horizon. I can't see most of it, just the leftover smoke trails. I can feel the sound barrier break overhead several times a day while bombs drop on a ruined landscape. Sometimes planes land on our base for a quick refuel, but I spend most of my time in the underground bunker built during the cold war. The Russian front lines are miles away from ours with nothing but craters in between us.

I again feel unneeded. The truth is that the ground troops stopped trying to fight weeks ago, leaving the air forces to fight it out in the sky. The only thing to do is spend all day every day in a bunker underground, maybe getting guard duty once in a blue moon. There is no real mission. We just sit in these tight concrete halls, waiting for the bombs to hit. Days pass in the dark. I get to go outside for twelve hour guard duty, if I'm lucky, only to hear the planes battle far above me. I can't tell how long I've been here. Rick would have known exactly how long we've been down here. I hear him sometimes, when the lights go out. He calls out to me, "Where are you?" I call back, "I'm here. Right here," but he can't hear me. I hate the dark.

I stare at the ruins of what was once a beautiful landscape. The sky erupts with roaring planes over head. Neither side ever reaches the bombing destinations. Never have to really worry about it, and if one gets through, I would never know. The explosion would kill me before I could care. I bet it would have been fun to fly.

"Jason, your shift's over!"

I turn to see Angel coming.

"Cool." I'm tired from being on guard duty for eight hours, but I don't want to go back into the dark bunker.

"Wait a second." Angel grabs the binoculars issued to the guards. "Holy shit, we have incoming!"

"Wha…?"

He grabs the radio. "We have tanks, hostiles incoming!"

I slap myself awake.

Meatball runs out, practically foaming at the mouth, "Finally some real action!"

An explosion destroys a guard post fifty yards from me.

I'm awake now and can feel the adrenaline pumping through my veins. I want to kill every last one of these bastards, for Rick.

We station ourselves in trenches around the outside of the base. The tanks look like older models from the cold war. Explosions erupt all around us. They can still fire. We are not prepared for this. Mounted guns open fire but have little effect. The tanks fire back, and I duck for cover as the mounted guns explode. "Call for air support!" but they're busy with their own battle. Meatball fires madly with his light machine gun, but might as well be using a BB gun.

Someone yells, "Fall back!"

I grab Meatball as he reloads. "Come on!"

We run, dirt from an explosion showers us. It's chaos, everyone running for their lives. Shit, shit, shit. We're going to die. We jump behind a concrete wall while the one next to us explodes. The shock shakes my core as the debris hits my skin. My eardrums rupture. All I can hear is a high pitch screech. I crawl away. There isn't enough cover to stand up. Another explosion throws more debris at me, and the shock waves shift my insides. I can't hear anything anymore.

I'll see you soon, Rick.

Angel, Luis, and a few others run up with rocket launchers. They fire on the tanks, destroying them. Just like that, it's over.

"Holy fucking shit!" My ears ring with constant pain. I throw off my helmet, take a huge drink of water, and pour the rest on my face. I feel the burn of many small cuts. I look at the smoldering tanks and see Meatball shooting the burnt corpse of a Russian who didn't make it out of the tank in time.

"How do you like that, you piece of shit! It doesn't feel so good to be on the other side! Does it? Ha!"

The tank burns for hours. We pile up the dead and unused ammo, take stock of it all. We lost four people. I never even learned their names. The Russians lost five T-55 tanks and twenty soldiers. I was right about the tanks being from the cold war.

Then it's back to normal, sitting in the dark underground as the action happens far above. Meatball talks endlessly about how awesome our fight was. I'm not going to lie, I was fucking terrified. My first real battle and I never fired a round. Why am I even here?

At least the darkness is here for me. Things stay quiet for a long time after that. At least until I get a letter from Zack.

Hey Jason,

We heard about Rick. It hit Alex and I really hard so I can't imagine what you're going through, but stay strong. We are still with you, even if we are on the other side of the world. A lot has happened for us on the USS Bush somewhere in the north pacific. The ship is named after the former president, but we never call the ship by its full name. It has been torpedoed and on fire three times since we got here but keeps on kicking. Alex has started wearing a helmet everywhere after hitting his head on every doorway. I have met a girl. Her name is Megan. She has the same job as me and we hit it off. I hope you get to meet her one day. She is amazing. One day we will all go home and we can say our goodbyes to Rick together.

Your friend always, Zack

P.S. Alex is also writing you a letter too, so stay tuned.

I'm glad they're doing fine and Zack is getting some action. Good for him. How do you go on a date on an aircraft carrier? Maybe we should have joined the navy with them. Would have been safer.

The darkness is comforting. There's nothing to worry about. Nothing at all. Until Angel grabs me and drags me for a poker game. "Come on, Mopey. You can't hide in the dark forever." He sits me at a table with Luis and three others.

Luis asks, "Is Mopey going to join us today?"

Angel smacks my back hard and says, "Damn right."

"Good. We are playing poker with aces high. Buy-in is whatever value you have."

I fish around in my pockets. What do I have? I pull out a crumpled up American dollar bill. "Will this work?"

Luis smiles with all his crooked teeth. "Sure will." I forgot how many fillings he has. "Let me introduce you. Gentlemen, this is Private First Class Mopey."

They say together, "Hi, Mopey."

"Mopey, say hello to Sergeant Anderson." He nods at a short man with a receding hairline and a thick mustache, then at a red haired man with no eyebrows. "Private Winters." Around the table to a bald man in aviator glasses and a Kevlar vest who doesn't smile. "Corporal Humphrey here is back from a classified mission. Don't ask 'cause he won't tell. And finally, our great Sergeant George McIntyre." A familiar face, another survivor from Cairo.

The game goes on for over an hour. Somehow every time I start to win, I lose it just as quick while Luis and Angel slowly gain everything. I think they're counting cards. They have to be, but that takes a lot of thought. Are they secret math geniuses?

I don't think I'm very good at this game, but it's become a matter of pride. I can't walk away until I make everything back, even if my buy-in was small. All I have left is a chocolate bar. I haven't seen one of these since deployment. It holds a high value in this game.

Then Meatball bursts in. "Sarge!"

George stays seated and calmly answers, "What is it, Private? Can't you see we're in the middle of something?"

"Shit has gone down! Sir."

George puts his cards face down on the table. "Calm down. What happened?"

"Russia invaded the US."

We all stop, look at each other and rush out of the room. I push past Meatball while Angel and Luis pocket their winnings. In the common room there is an old TV with the news playing. Everyone is gathered around, talking during the commercial break. George makes his way to the front.

I try to sneak in close behind, but the gap closes too quick. CNN returns.

"Everyone shut up!"

We go silent.

"Continuing with our top story. At approximately two a.m. last night, after a lengthy naval battle with Russian forces, we've lost the US naval fleet in the northern Pacific. Now the Russian naval fleet has landed on the shores of Alaska. With new information coming in, it appears Russian forces are currently making their way through US soil."

What US ships were in the battle? I have a deep sinking feeling in my gut.

They won't say on the news, but someone has to know. I bet someone in military intelligence does. I run at a full sprint to intelligence, knocking people out of my way as I go. Someone calls me an asshole. I don't care if I get chewed out for it. I need to know what ships sank. The door isn't locked and I burst in. They're in a frantic state of reading papers and yelling at each other.

I grab the nearest person. "What ships sank in the invasion?"

He pushes me away. "Don't touch me, private, or I will have you court-martialed."

"I'm sorry, but I need to know. Was the *USS Bush* involved? Please, I have friends out there!" I don't hide the desperation in my voice.

"Listen, Private"—he looks at the name on my uniform—"Baker, information is still coming in. We don't know yet." He clearly doesn't want to waste anymore time with me.

I take out the chocolate bar I just won and give it to him. "Please, I need to know if the *USS Bush* sank in the battle."

He quickly looks both ways, pocketing the treat. "Come find me in an hour."

I walk out, lean against the wall, and sink to the ground. I sit there and think about the last time we were all together. Our first taste of hard liquor. I need you guys. Please don't leave me too. Everything slows down until Mr. Intelligence comes out.

I shoot up, "Well?"

He sighs. "I'm sorry."

My heart sinks as it dawns on me that I'm all that's left. All my friends are gone. I want to think about the last time we were together drinking Snake Bite, but all I feel is empty.

"The *USS Bush* sank after splitting in half from a new kind of thermite bomb. With those frozen waters, don't count on any survivors." As he walks away, I hear the sound of a candy bar wrapper being torn.

That's it then. I'm all that's left.

"Jason!"

I turn around to see Meatball in a rush. "Grab your gear, we're moving out."

I guess there isn't much else to do... Wait a second. "Meatball, when the hell did you become a corporal?"

He puffs out his chest. "Oh, about twenty minutes ago. And as an officer, it is my job to lead my squad."

"Don't get your head too far up your own ass. You're a noncommissioned officer, Corporal Meatball."

Still smiling, he says, "Well, Private Mopey, we are moving out, so get your shit together." He runs off.

I go to my quarters and pack up my stuff.

Angel and Luis are already there. Angel says, "It's fucking bullshit is what it is."

Calmly, Luis says, "Well, what did you expect? A medal of honor? A promotion to general? A blowjob from Uncle Sam?"

Angel says, "No, but for him to get promoted over us is fucking bullshit. We're the reason everyone survived that battle."

Luis says, "Again, what did you expect? Were both convicts and giving us credit makes everyone else look bad."

Angel throws his pack over his shoulder with all his force. "He didn't do a goddamn thing." He looks over at me. "Jason, what did you and Meatball even do in the fight with the tanks?"

I say, "We ran away and tried not to die. I did temporarily lose my hearing, but that's it." The honest truth. "Is this about Meatball's promotion?"

"No shit, genius. What else would it be about? That little shit didn't do anything while me and Luis gathered people to storm the armory and get the anti-tank weapons that saved everyone. But we don't get any medals or promotions. That's fucking bullshit!" Clearly pissed off, he grabs the rest of his gear and storms out.

I yell to him, "Don't forget your sword."

He storms back in and grabs it. "Thank you." And storms back out.

That is bullshit. Angel organized troops in combat

during a losing battle and led us to victory. That is as good a reason as any to promote someone. Instead, they gave it to Meatball who did just as much as me, and I ran for dear life. I'm not even ashamed of it. What the hell could one person with an assault rifle do to a squadron of five fucking tanks? Even if the tanks seemed like relics from the cold war.

CHAPTER 11

THE ENTIRE TRIP FEELS AWKWARD. Not because we're going to a front with the highest casualties. Instead, it's anger focused on Meatball. The entire platoon believes Angel should have gotten the promotion. First Sergeant McIntyre wanted Angel to be promoted. McIntyre has found Meatball to be annoying since Egypt. Nothing I can do about it, so I think about home and remembering all the good times my friends and I had. It hasn't even been a year and they're all dead.

"Why are we going south? Wouldn't it make more sense to invade Russia through Turkey?"

"Well, as corporal—"

There it is, the new promotion has already gone to his head.

"—I was informed that the European militaries have already pushed through Moscow. And with the help of the Canadian military, the Russian invasion is being halted in Alaska. We're needed in Iran against the Chinese, where the real fight is."

To shut up Meatball, McIntyre says, "We're being sent

to face the remaining Chinese forces in and around the city of Baghdad. Iran has been in a constant tug of war between the US and the Chinese. Recently, India cut off future Chinese support from the sea and are engaging in land battles in the Tibetan region. According to all accounts, Iran has had massive death tolls on every side."

We pass by shanty towns of locals that had to evacuate the city. Children run by our trucks begging for food. I don't have any to give them. I see adults with rotting bandages sitting in mud. Everything reeks of shit and rot. The cost of this fight has taken everything from these people. An old woman throws mud at our truck and curses us, then falls to the ground crying until a child helps her up. I feel pity, but there's nothing I can really do for her.

As we march in, the old guard shambles out. They're black from dirt and stained with blood. They carry out wounded, but every last one of them looks beat to hell. The battalion was cut to a fifth its original size.

Someone yells, "Welcome to The Grinder, cherries!"

So that's what real combat looks like.

Our base camp is a converted warehouse with concrete walls topped with razor wire. There are dusty, ragged tents everywhere and various vehicles set up with mounted guns as a moving parameter guard. I walk by the medical tent and hear the screams of pain from the injured. Medical staff do their best to treat what they can, but the only real hope is a helicopter evacuation to a military hospital miles away. Our platoon's tent is completely empty. I already miss the cots from Egypt, but at least we have some cover from the elements.

We're split into squads to clear buildings. The Chinese

advanced during the battalion's exchange and dug in deep. Our job is to find and destroy the enemy, as well as retake the city. The higher ups don't want to bomb the city. The reason I am given by our commanding officer, Major Hugo, is to keep the civilians on our side. "We want there to be something left after this war." The other reason, I am told by a veteran of the battle, "It's pride. The US has spent so much time and money here that it would go against their investment and soldiers are disposable cannon fodder."

So we do it the old fashioned way, one building at a time. Sergeant McIntyre leads us. He was absent during the tank fight in Turkey and acts like he has something to prove now. "Don't hug the walls too tight, stay spread out."

At the edge of the city, the fighting starts. Bursts of gunfire flash from high windows. We take cover and fire back. A bullet zings past my head, the shock wave making me jump a bit. I duck behind a wall and then open fire at the flashes of light. Grenades explode from the widows. Then just as suddenly, the gun shots stop. I guess we got them.

We storm the first building, escaping the chaos of the street. Meatball rushes forward too quickly to properly clear any rooms. Luis taps me on the shoulder. He's got my back, and Angel has his. I have to watch Meatball's back. Of course I get the most difficult job.

Gunfire erupts on the floor above me.

"Shit!"

We run up the stairs, finding Meatball pinned down behind a broken door. I can't get a clear shot.

"Covering fire!" I fire blindly at the enemy knowing I won't hit anything, but they will take cover.

Meatball uses the opening to throw a grenade. Shrapnel and red mist burst from the enemies' position.

Meatball yells, "We have them on the run now," and charges farther up the stairs.

"Wait! You idiot!"

But he's not listening. Only thinking about earning medals. Unless he gets himself killed because he doesn't properly clear the damn building.

Meatball runs past a room as the door opens and then a Chinese soldier steps out. Our eyes meet. I drop to my knee as he fires his QBZ from the hip. I squeeze the trigger, firing a short burst of three rounds into his chest. He drops, as I hear a series of thuds behind me. I turn to see Luis tumbling down the stairs. Angel yells for his friend. I check the room for anyone else. Clear. I run down the stairs to Angel and Luis. He's unconscious and his arm is bleeding.

Angel yells, "That fucking idiot! I swear I'm going to kill him."

I give him a quick jab to his body armor. "Focus! We have to get Luis out of here."

"But if that idiot had done his job—"

"Well, he didn't! We have to deal with it now."

Angel ties a bandage around Luis's wound, stopping the bleeding.

"Can you carry him?" Luis and Angel are about the same size. We could easily carry him together, but I don't want to leave Meatball here even if he is an idiot.

Angel says, "I've got him. I would hate to have to come back here for another body." We lift Luis on to Angel's back. With a quick nod to show that Luis is secure, Angel hurries out.

I clear each and every room as fast as I can without overlooking anything. There is no one else anywhere. Then I hear gunfire above me. What kind of trouble are you in now, Meatball? I reach the roof to find Meatball firing his light machine gun at the neighboring building and laughing out insults. He's enjoying himself. This feels wrong. He is like a wild animal enjoying a kill for sport. I wait until he runs out of ammo, afraid he might shoot me as a reaction if I say anything.

His gun runs dry, and as he starts to reload, I yell, "Meatball! What the fuck?!"

He spins around ready to fire, his face twisted into a cruel smile.

I was right, but he can't fire an empty gun.

Still smiling, Meatball says, "Jason! Good news! I cleared the building next to us." He starts reloading. "Where are the others?"

I slowly walk forward, feeling like I'm approaching a rabid animal. "Luis got hit and Angel took him back. We need to do the same."

He stops reloading. "I suppose you're right. I'm running low anyway."

As he passes me, he starts to whistle a cheerful tune.

I cautiously move to the edge of the building where Meatball was shooting. I'm afraid of what I might see but look over anyway. There are civilian bodies and maybe one or two Chinese soldiers scattered beyond the broken windows. I feel sick to my stomach. Did I just let him kill a bunch of innocent people? No, I can't think like that. I didn't know what he was shooting at. For all I know, the civilians were already dead and Meatball only hit the enemy. But that look on his face…he could have. I don't have any proof, and I have to live with that.

I double check the building on my way out. I went so fast to catch up to Meatball though, I could have missed something. As I leave the building, a sniper team heads in. They will be on overwatch during the night.

As I rejoin the fight on the streets, I feel relieved that the building is clear. Then I immediately feel overwhelmed looking at how many buildings are left to fight through. This is going to take forever.

When we get back to base camp hours later, I am exhausted. I ran through over a dozen buildings and fired so many rounds at possible targets, though I have no idea how many I hit. We pass the next shift as they leave to hold our position through the night.

The instant we walk through the gates, Angel greets Meatball with a punch to the face. "You fucking idiot!"

I immediately jump in between the two of them and several others grab Angel. "Hey! We don't need this!" Not my best line, but it just came out.

Meatball looks stunned. I can't tell if he's afraid or angry.

Angel shoves everyone off of him. "If you ever go Rambo like that again and put us at risk, I will fucking kill you."

Meatball looks around for support, but no one is really on his side.

Don't expect any, Meatball. I stayed in between them. I wanted to punch Meatball too, but that wouldn't accomplish anything.

He grumbles profanity under his breath and walks away.

Everyone else disperses, leaving me alone with Angel. "So, Angel, how's Luis?"

Still watching Meatball walk away, he says, "He'll be fine. The arm wound was just a scratch. His body armor absorbed the rest of the damage. He'll be off the line for a week or two because of the concussion he got falling down the stairs."

"Well, that's good at least, but you might get court-martialed for hitting a superior officer."

"Doubt it. No one saw a thing." Aside from the couple of soldiers who jumped up to stop him, no one seemed to care. Sergeant McIntyre was clearly looking in the opposite direction and where's the lieutenant? In fact, no one of significant rank is anywhere to be seen.

We're rationed out MREs. I get Minestrone with crackers and packed peanut butter. The powdered coffee mix in the pack is bitter, but I feel some energy return. It all tastes kind of bland, but not bad, like a cheap knock off brand of the good stuff.

Five dead and seven wounded, including Luis. I guess we got the easy buildings. We are ordered to dig in for the night in case the Chinese launch a counteroffensive. I'm given the first watch because I finished my meal first and issued night vision goggles. Watching the street from the second floor, everything looks clear, but at any moment there could be a counterattack.

Holy shit! I killed someone today. That was the first time I fired my weapon and I killed someone. I feel…. I don't really know. It was a moment of adrenaline. I saved myself and protected my friends. I'm glad about that, but for the most part, I don't really feel much of anything. It was kind of easy. Almost too easy. So that's what it means to kill? I expected more, but I feel nothing.

"Jason, your shift is over." I know this guy, but I'm so bad with names.

"It's all yours, Vic." Got it right.

I hand him the night vision goggles.

"Thanks." He lights up a cigarette and hands me the pack.

"No, I don't smoke."

Looking at me in the slight glow from his lighter, he says, "You're still pumped up from the fight earlier." He pulls out a cigarette from the pack. "Trust me, this will help you calm down."

I hesitate, so he lights it for me. The smoke hits my lungs and I start coughing. Why the hell did I just do that? I fight to catch my breath. Then I feel euphoric and everything calms down for just a second. I take another drag, cough a bit. Then the calmness sinks deeper.

Vic smiles. "You guys got to Turkey after the real fighting stopped. I remember my first fight. I was so stressed out afterward, I couldn't sleep. Every day we fought through the rubble as bombs dropped on us. I thought there was no end. Until a friend offered me a cigarette, saying it would calm me down. It sure as hell does." He chuckles a bit. "They hammered it into us as kids that this will kill you." He holds out the burning bud. "But I doubt it will kill me before someone else does."

We look out into the city as the lights of a distant raging battle flicker.

"Might as well find something that brings comfort in this shit show." He takes a long drag from his cigarette before putting it out.

CHAPTER 12

NOTHING HAPPENED IN THE SECOND platoon's sector. Fourth platoon got ambushed. The Chinese snuck in and slit ten people's throats with bayonets. We were woken up because someone started shooting, but the damage was already done. That could have just as easily been our sector. It will be a long time until replacements come and there's a city to take. We go back out as the other battalion comes in. In order to keep the pressure on the enemy, we switch between the two battalions. One goes on the attack while the other resupplies and rests, but the intervals feel a bit short.

On day two, I wake up with a headache from the cigarette and a pain in my back from sleeping on the ground. There's no time to complain though. We have to go fight. I wish I saved some of that coffee mix to wake me up.

We march back into the city and are greeted with snipers pinning us down. I dive behind a building for cover as we try to pinpoint where they are.

Sergeant McIntyre yells to me, "Jason! One's in your building. Sixth floor, north side!"

I look around for a way in.

There's a wooden door. Angel pats my shoulder and hands me a breaching explosive. We blow the door open. The explosion catches me off guard. I must have set off a boobytrap. We clear the bottom floor. It's empty. Second floor, empty. Third and fourth floor, clear. We are getting close to the sniper. I pull the pin on a grenade and cook it for three seconds, not wanting it thrown back, then toss it to the fifth floor. There is a short scream of pain mixed into the explosion. I switch my rifle to full auto, and we storm the fifth floor. No unnecessary thoughts. I squeeze the trigger, taking down anything that moves. Bodies drop as I keep pushing up the stairs. I drop my magazine, slam in a new one, and release the catch. I kick open the last door, and with no hesitation, fill the sniper with hot lead.

"Clear!"

Angel yells back, "Clear!"

That escalated quickly. I went so long without firing my weapon, to killing ten people in a few minutes. We return to the street battle and keep fighting.

By day three, there's hardly enough time to take a proper shit before we're sent back to the fight. The boot camp time limit makes sense now. There's even more fighting on the street this time. A machine gun pins us down behind a corner. Angel pulls the pin on a grenade, and the second the gunner stops to reload, he throws it. The floor explodes, and we press forward. Progress is slow. Every building is full of Chinese soldiers who refuse to give up. One runs out of ammo and charges us with his bayonet in one hand and a grenade in the other. We cut him down quickly, but he gets too close for comfort. His dead body falls on the grenade, and the explosion sends chunks of human remains at us. Hours pass and it starts to get dark. We switch out with the other battalion. We'll get the night shift soon.

It's a quiet night with no advances. "I need to take a piss. Anyone else?" Always travel with a battle buddy, so some kid, I think his name is Nick, volunteers. We leave the safety of the building to piss outside.

Nick asks, "Where are you from?"

A fair question. "I'm from—"

Flares light the dark world.

I yell, "Get down," dropping to the floor.

Tracer rounds hit all around us. Nick falls limp next to me. The flare light shines on the hollowed out remains of his face. He was dead before he hit the ground. I cower behind his corpse as more incoming rounds pelt his lifeless body. Everyone else returns fire. I'm stuck in the middle of a fire fight with a dead ally as my only cover. An hour passes before the shooting calms down.

"Jason! Are you still out there?"

We drag the lifeless body of Nick back to friendly lines. Leave no man behind.

By day six, it's all just like any other day. I resupply, but I'm not hungry this time. I just want a cigarette and coffee. I trade some of my MRE for a pack of smokes but keep the instant coffee mix. It's arguably the only thing keeping me going. I start to get comfortable when it's our turn to switch. God damn it, there's never enough time.

Sergeant McIntyre tells us to maintain fire control. "Don't want to hit a friendly in the dark."

But I have a feeling it's to conserve ammo. This is a siege. We not only have to beat the enemy, we have to *outlast* them. Whoever exhausts their supplies first loses. Progress is slower at night, but I fire less bullets. It feels like we're winning. We are pushing deeper into the city, but I'm tired. I just want to sleep, but we keep fighting.

We switch just before the sun comes up on day seven. I resupply, but I don't need as much. None of us do. I eat some grub. Crunchy bread or some kind of cracker, I can't tell which. We also get a small packet of peanut butter, which I am slowly building a dislike for. We will have this city soon, and I start to fall into a deep sleep only to be woken up by a rude kick from Sergeant McIntyre, telling me to return to the fight. As I pass the other platoon, I notice their numbers have shrunk significantly and most of them are wounded.

I grab a private who isn't badly hurt. "What happened?"

The look behind his eyes are of a broken man. "They attacked us like fucking animals, man."

They had been pushed back to where we started, like all our progress was meaningless.

We make no progress. Hell, we barely hold the line. I have to carry Vic back. His left leg was blown off. He got lucky the explosion partly cauterized the wound shut. Otherwise, he would have bled to death. He's heavy, but he'll get to go home. I say goodbye, resupply, eat something that's legally food with a peanut butter packet, and pass out. Only to be kicked awake again to go fight. I hate this. I smoke a cigarette to calm myself.

By day twelve, I've stopped using automatic firing or even burst fire. I only use a single shot and only fire at targets I can hit. The less bullets I use, the less time I spend resupplying. Mid-fight, my stomach gives me a mean kick.

It was only a matter of time before the food rations decided to fight me as well.

When we get relieved, we pass the other battalion with a bunch of fresh-faced kids. They have no idea what's coming.

"Have fun, cherries!" Meatball yells.

I don't have time to think as I rush to the designated shitter, which is just a glorified hole. Relief, but of course, there's no toilet paper. I reach into my bag and grab my secret supply. Thank you, Dad. I notice a bunch of tiny holes in my uniform from the fight. I had no idea I had this many close calls. I clean up and resupply. I don't eat most of the MRE anymore. I would rather smoke and drink some coffee. Why do so many of them have peanut butter in them? I try to trade, but everyone feels the same about peanut butter by now.

I sit down next to Angel. "Have you gotten any kills with that sword yet?" His katana rests on his back, ready to be pulled at any moment.

Angel says, "Not yet, but soon. I can feel it."

I joke, "I'm sure your ninja senses are very keen."

He makes a ridiculous karate gesture, saying, "Damn right. I'm the great Mexican ninja warrior."

I say, "I'm not calling you that."

He says, "If you say so, Private Mopey."

By fourteen days of rotation after rotation, every time we gain ground, we are losing it in the next change. We get new replacement soldiers, but they are just a bunch of kids fresh from boot camp. I'm somewhere around five months in, I think, and still eighteen years old, but feel so much older than these kids. I have more kills on my hands than I care to count.

I hear these cherries talk of big games. "I can't wait to get some action."

I tell them, "Shut the fuck up and try not to get shot." They shut up after their first rotation, if they live. Otherwise, I have to carry their corpse out, then resupply and try to sleep.

Luis returns and it feels like it could be a good day, but the rain comes and makes the ground muddy, cuts down our visibility, and brings a fresh smell of decay from the dead not collected. After the rotation, we have to find a dry spot to clean our guns, cutting into our already short sleep schedule.

"You picked a bad day to come back, Luis."

He shrugs. "There are only bad days."

I hate that he's right.

He shows us the scar on his arm. Impressive, but I'm jealous of his clean new uniform. Everyone else is wearing torn rags. This rain is the closest thing to a shower we've had since we got here. I would kill for a warm shower and a hot meal without peanut butter.

"Welcome back to The Shit, my friend."

We press into the city on day sixteen, and I get the first kill of the day within minutes. This enemy was setting a trip wire. No one saw the landmine ten yards away until it was too late and blew three friends to nothing. I may not know everyone's names, but it still hurts to lose fellow troops. In the end, we had to retreat. They hit us with grands and lured us into a minefield. I did learn the Chinese word for grenade. At least, I think. They yelled, "Shǒuliúdàn" every time a grenade was thrown.

With the rain blocking the sun for a while, I have lost track of the days. We fight, lose more people, and come back bloody and muddy. Something small got me good in the calf. I don't even know where it came from in the chaos. I just felt a sudden sting. I get my leg cleaned and patched up by our medic. It's not bad enough to get me off the line though. However, I do feel lucky to have only gotten a scratch while Malcolm, a man who had been with this battalion before I was transferred, got hit in the spine. He lost a lot of blood and might not make it. If he does, he'll never walk again. That could have easily been me. Luck is a bitch, and she runs out eventually.

There's less ammo available this time. We must be running low. I want to be done here. I need a cigarette. I find a dry place to keep my leg elevated. Last thing I need is an infection, but that could get me sent home. However, I don't want to have my leg sawed off. Meatball is cleaning his gun and muttering to himself. I'm worried about him.

Luis and Angel start up a game of cards with some others. One of the new replacements is called Marv, I think, and Luis keeps calling the other guy Dick. Is that his name or just a mean nickname? I just don't care enough to figure it out. There's no point learning anyone's name when they first get here. Most replacements die within a few days of arrival.

I receive another rude awakening to go back out and ask Luis what they won this time.

He smiles and says, "A brand new pair of socks."

"You son of a bitch!" I would kill for a new pair of socks. My socks are beat to shit, and we rarely get new ones. I'm half tempted to steal those, but I hold it down. "I'll trade you a roll of TP for those."

Not expecting that, he thinks for a moment. "Deal."

We exchange.

Good deal. I have another fresh roll hidden away in my emergency stack and Luis got fresh socks with his new uniform anyway.

I carry Marv's corpse off the line. We leave no man behind. We got the farthest into the city than we ever had today. Marv was so proud of how much ass we were kicking until a sniper got him in the head. It looked quick. I drop him into the pile of all the other corpses that will be shipped home. The pile is large, too many faces to remember. Marv was fresh out of high school, with his whole life ahead of him, and now he's just another corpse in the pile. I'm only a few months older than him, but I feel so very old. I care so much less now. I feel so very little. I need ammo and supplies. Besides he doesn't need them anymore. I want to survive. I don't want to go home in a plastic bag, so I take his unused ammo, rations, socks and water. I will survive.

CHAPTER 13

'M KICKED AWAKE. "GOD FUCKING damn it. Alright, give me a second."

Angel shushes me.

Feeling insulted, I tell him to go fuck himself.

He shushes me again. "Listen, something isn't right." All the gunfire had stopped. "There's a whisper in the wind."

Confused, I ask, "Did we win?"

Angel says, "No, the other shift has gone silent."

The whisper grows the faintest bit louder.

"What is that?"

Angel says, "It sounds like a chant."

I feel uneasy. I think we all do. Sergeant McIntyre starts barking orders at us to take up defensive positions. The chant grows louder. I can almost hear it clearly but don't know what it is. It's something in Chinese.

Gunfire and explosions erupt from the front lines deep in the city. Desperate cries for support scream on the radio. A quick squeal of pain followed by a thud and the radio goes silent. Our fresh captain, excited for glory, orders us to deploy. He can't be more than twenty-two. That position has been emptied twice since I got here, so I chose not to learn his name. We don't hesitate to jump to action. We won't abandon our brothers in arms. We have been fighting for this city together.

We rush down the war torn street, the smell of death and shit staining my nostrils. The distant gunfire falls silent. We slow down, moving from one defensive position to the next. The chanting starts up again, far louder than before. A primal fear hits me, and my hair stands on end. They are coming.

The chant grows louder. They're right on top of us. They have to be on the next street over. We turn the corner, and there in battle formation stand thousands of Chinese soldiers with fixed bayonets. The chant turns into a battle cry as they charge us. We open fire.

Automatic fire keeps them at bay for thirty seconds. It's not long enough. They have the larger force with a do or die will. This has to be their last stand. As soon as our guns run dry, they are upon us. They cut through those in front, trampling their bodies as they charge. A handful of light machine guns keep firing, but it's not enough. They just keep coming.

"Fall back!"

Not caring who said it, I run, reloading as I go and then firing blindly as I retreat. I turn back around the corner, heading back to base camp. I have to get out of here.

Angel grabs me, yelling, "Hold the line!"

The sudden stop catches me off guard. I realize I would never make it back to base camp before they overtake me. Not everyone stops. At least a dozen fellow troops keep running away. I will stay with the last of Beta Company.

We regroup up the street, making a firing line three rows

deep. First row is all the remaining light machine gunners on their stomachs, second row is rifle men with grenade launchers on one knee, and the final row is standing rifle men.

Angel yells, "Make every shot count!" as he raises his sword in the air.

The Chinese turn the corner.

"Hold!"

I almost pull the trigger but focus on slowing my breathing.

The enemy gets less than fifty yards from us.

Stay calm, I can do this.

"First row...*fire*!" Angel swings down his sword, unleashing a wall of continuous bullets.

They keep coming with no sign of retreat. Forty yards.

First row runs dry.

"Second row! *Fire*!" Grenades explode, painting the road with blood.

They climb over the piles of their dead comrades. Thirty yards.

"Third row! *Fire*!"

We cut down so many, but it's still not enough.

Twenty yards.

We run dry as the first row starts firing again.

They're right in front of us.

In the fraction of a second that the light machine guns run dry, the remains of the horde overtake us. Angel lets out a battle cry, swinging his sword, slicing his enemies head clean off.

I empty my magazine. My gun runs dry as the butt of a gun smacks me in the jaw. I feel teeth dislodge. Adrenalin fills my veins. I immediately grab him and push my shoulder into him, using his momentum against him to hip toss him onto the hard ground. Then I stomp on his throat with all the hatred I have. He lets out a painful gasp, and I stomp again as a sharp pain jolts through my other leg. I swing my gun like a bat at the fucker who just stabbed my ass. The impact crumples him to the ground. I lift my gun high in the air and swing down like a hammer. His skull cracks open.

No unnecessary thoughts. Only rage and the will to live.

I get tackled and turn as a knife is about to be stabbed into my chest. I put out my hand to stop it but misjudge the distance. The blade pierces through my palm, but I keep the blade from hitting the rest of me. His other hand wraps around my throat and squeezes. I don't try to break the choke. Instead, I shove fingers into his eyes. He takes his hand off my throat to stop me, but I press harder until I feel the pop of his eyeballs. I use his instability to roll him off. My hand is still caught on his knife. I rip my fingers out of his eye sockets. Blood spurts out, and he's screaming in pain. I grab a large rock and slam the clump down, hearing his skull crack. I slam down again and his head splits.

With my hand in the air about to come down for my fourth hit, I see Angel break the tip of his sword on an enemy's rifle and then stab the broken sword into his opponent without hesitation. His form is unbelievable. Either he's diligently trained without us ever knowing or he was a great swordsman in a previous life.

I also see a Chinese soldier charging at me with his bayonet and try to dodge, but I don't get out of the way fast enough. The blade stabs me just under my left collarbone. I grab the gun barrel in a desperate attempt to stop it from going in farther. I fail as he pushes me to the ground. The blade sinks up to the hilt. I feel it pop out the other side.

"Mother *fucker*!" Shit! I need to do something.

The knife is still in my left hand. Still holding the barrel, I kick him between his legs as hard as I can. He crumples but still holds onto his rifle. I pull the blade out of my palm and start stabbing wildly. I stab his hands, then his arms, until he lets go of the gun. My shoulder screams in agony, but I keep stabbing. I press closer, stabbing into his gut. He tries to stop me, but his bloody hands can't get a solid grip. Face to face, he chokes up blood. I see the regret in his eyes. I pull out my knife, then stab his neck, ripping his throat open. Blood gushes out, dousing me.

Everyone has devolved into hand to hand combat. We're holding the last of them. Angel cuts down opponents left and right with a broken sword.

Someone yells, "shǒuliúdàn," followed by several other Chinese soldiers. Pins are pulled and grenades released.

I use a corpse as a shield.

Explosions erupt everywhere.

CHAPTER 14

"**F**UCK!" EVERYTHING HURTS.

I disconnect the bayonet from the rifle. If I pull it out, I will bleed to death. I stumble as best I can to my rifle. One handed, I drop the empty magazine and slam in my last one. Everything is still. I can only hear my own heartbeat.

Just breathe, catch your breath.

Everyone is dead. Bodies everywhere. The entire company is dead, and I look back up the street where piles of Chinese soldiers lie motionless.

"Ahhhhh!" a Chinese soldier yells as he pulls his knife out of Sergeant McIntyre's chest.

Our eyes meet, his glow like a feral animal while mine are cold. I put two rounds through his chest before he can take a step.

I yell, "Who's not dead, sound off?" My jaw hurts. I feel something loose and spit out a molar.

"Over here!" a familiar voice yells.

I try to stand, but my leg seizes and I fall over. "Fucking

shit." I use my rifle as a cane, keeping my hand on the handle and my finger near the trigger. Fuck, everything hurts.

Luis is tending to Angel, doing his best to stop the bleeding from what looks like a dozen wounds. "Stay with me, damn it." His voice is desperate. He's bleeding from a large cut on his head, a gash in his side, and some kind of leg wound. I can't tell if his arms had been damaged due to all the gushing blood.

Luis yells, "Medic!"

No one answers. We're all that's left. We need evac now. I stumble to Sergeant McIntyre's body, each step pure agony, then fall over as I reach for the radio. He had been stabbed so many times, his chest looks like crushed raspberries. Not the time to think of food.

"This is Private First Class Baker of Beta Company requesting immediate evac."

They respond quickly, "We read you. We already have a convoy heading to your last known location."

Thank God… Wait, how do they already know?

It doesn't take me long to remember the bunch of soldiers that ran when Angel tried to rally everyone. Meatball was running the fastest. I am both mad and relieved. I'm mad because if they had stayed to fight, then we could have held them back longer and we might not have been overrun. However, I'm relieved because now we can evac. I yell the good news over to Luis and Angel.

I have to stop my bleeding before I bleed to death. Not far from McIntyre are the remains of our medic. I wrap up my hand as best I can. The wound in my left ass cheek is a bit tougher, but I get it. I pad cloth around the bayonet still in my shoulder. The slightest touch sends a jolt of pain through my entire body. It hurts so bad I want to puke. I tighten the tourniquet using my one good arm and my teeth. It hurts, but I refuse to bleed out after surviving all this.

Luis's desperate voice yells, "I can't stop the bleeding."

God damn it.

"We have to get Angel to a medic now!"

I know what he means, but I don't want to move. I have to fight the weight of gravity with every ounce of strength I have left. Finally, I stand once again and make my way back to them with the medic's bag on my good shoulder. When a hand grabs my left leg, the sudden stop sends a jolt of pain throughout my entire body. I look down at a Chinese soldier choking on his own blood. His eye's burn with hate. Without saying a word, I put my gun to his head and pull the trigger. His head explodes and his hand goes limp. I keep pushing myself forward.

Luis is doing his best to pick up Angel, but he can't with all his wounds. Angel is barely breathing. I get on his left side while Luis takes the right.

Angel faintly says, "I feel cold."

He's lost too much blood, so we start walking.

"You're going to be fine. We'll get patched up and they'll give you a medal. And promote you straight to lieutenant," I say to encourage my friend and also to keep myself going.

Two wounded men carrying an almost dead man. We look like two friends carrying a drunken buddy home from the bar. I wish that's what we were doing, but none of us are even old enough to drink.

Time starts to move slowly. All the buildings look the same. I'm starting to feel cold. I can't stop. I have to keep going. Angel would do the same for us. My feet feel heavy.

My leg feels numb except for the piercing pain in my ass. I can feel the exact spot on the lower part of my left ass cheek. Why the fuck did he stab me there, of all the places he could have gotten me? My back was wide open. He could have pierced my spine and killed me, but no! He got me on my left ass cheek. Mother fucker! It hurts so much to walk.

I can't focus on that. I have to focus on getting us back to base camp. Things are getting blurry. Oh no, that's a bad sign. I can't hold this much weight in my condition. Come on! Don't you dare give up now! However, gravity is a cruel bitch and she smacks me to the ground. I faintly hear Luis yelling at me, but he's so far away.

Oh God, I'm dying. Is this really it? After everything, I die here like this? All I got was eighteen years. I don't want to die. I want to go home. I want to see my family again. Mom, you taught me kindness, but you weren't afraid to fight back. Dad, you always found humor in everything. I'm sorry I wasn't strong enough. I'm sorry for everything.

Light fades into darkness. Everything feels so pointless. Voices yell out, calling me to them. Come back to us, they yell.

"Rick? Is that you?"

A sharp jolt of pain rushes through my body. Air enters my lungs for what feels like the first time.

"We have a pulse!"

There's a long tube going down my throat and everyone's yelling.

"O negative stat!"

Everything hurts again. It was better the other way. All the pain was gone. I try to lift my hand, but it feels so heavy. I feel something small stab me in the leg and the pain begins to fade again. Much better. My eyes feel heavy, until blackness returns.

I see home, and we're playing soccer. Alex passes the ball to Rick, and he kicks it to me. I have a clear shot at the goal. The field is on fire, burning yellow smoke. We have to take cover. Rick grabs my shoulder.

"Ow! That hurts man."

Blood bursts from his eyes. "I'll be waiting."

I pull back to see a bayonet in my shoulder.

My eyes open. I'm on my side with something solid propping me up in a soft bed with soft sheets.

"Welcome back, sleeping Mopey." Good to hear a familiar voice.

"With all the time you had, that's the best name you could come up with?" It kind of hurts to talk.

"Nope, thought it up on the spot." He's lying through his missing teeth.

"Luis, you're such a liar. I bet you spent days thinking of that line. Where are we anyway?"

"A military hospital in Kuwait. The food ain't half bad and some of the nurses aren't too bad looking either." Almost sounds like heaven.

"Where's Angel?"

Luis goes silent, speaking volumes.

Oh, please no, not him too.

Holding back a cry, Luis says, "He didn't make it."

Those words cut deeper than any of my stab wounds.

"They're sending his body home with the Distinguished Service Medal and a promotion to captain."

They only recognized his greatness in death.

CHAPTER 15

THE DOCTORS ARE STRETCHED EXTREMELY thin, but one eventually explains my condition to me. He's skinny, definitely not eating enough. There are dark shadows under his eyes. Reminds me of Pete. He looks at my chart. "Multiple stab wounds, but no vital organs were damaged. You're very lucky, Private Baker. You should be fully recovered in a month or two."

I ask, "Does that mean I'll be going home?"

He sighs like he's heard that question a hundred times before. "Unfortunately, that's not my call to make."

"Wait, but—"

"Based upon how well you recover and how much time is left in your deployment, Colonel Salois will decide where you will be sent." Then he leaves before I can say anything else.

Luis chuckles. "He said the same thing to me when I woke up."

I ask, "Where did you get hit?" Straining my neck, I look over at Luis.

He's covered in bandages. "Nothing too bad, just a

bunch of good cuts here and there. Four missing teeth, but the worst was on my side." Luis leans to show the bandage above his right hip. "The fucker got me real good in the appendix. Apparently though, it was unneeded."

"I wouldn't say various cuts so nonchalantly. Both your arms are entirely wrapped in bandages all the way from your shoulder to your fingertips."

He looks at his hands. "I guess we both lucked out." Wiggling them at me he says, "At least I still have all ten."

I spend over a week in bed before I feel strong enough to try walking. I can't use a wheelchair because I can't sit yet. I can only use one crutch because my left side got all the abuse, so I hobble as best I can the fifteen feet to the bathroom. There's not enough staff to help everyone, and if I used a bedpan, no one would clean it for hours. So I had to figure it out myself. I have to half squat awkwardly above the rim. Thank God, I still have my right hand. It's awkward washing my hand, but at least it's functional.

Luis's leg wound isn't as bad, and he's able to move around just fine. If the staff forgets to feed us, he brings food. One time he found a couple of potatoes. I did not know they could be eaten raw, and they have an odd crunch to them.

Everything hurts. The pain never leaves. There's hardly enough pain meds to go around. If we're really lucky, we might get a refill of pain killers, but the quality varies. Usually it's simple drug store painkillers like Advil. We pray for more oxycodone to take it all away, but it's so rare. It's worse at night. I can't sleep because of the pain, so I lay here wondering what was the point of any of it. Why did I get to live while so many died? Am I just here to suffer and watch everyone die? Just make the pain go away, but it won't. It is my burden to bear.

There are a few others in this room with us. Like Dallas who had his right arm blown off by artillery and always asks for a hand, finding it ironic. There's Phil who lost an eye and says he lost it when he saw an alien ship. Phil loves talking about aliens and can go on for hours about how they have been watching us for decades and now that we are distracted, they will attack us soon. Phil spends most of the time talking to Gabe. Poor Gabe got hit in the throat and can't talk back. We're all relatively low maintenance patents, which is why they forget about us sometimes. I'm not happy about it, but I understand why. There are just too many injured and not enough staff.

The only thing to do is watch television on an old TV set. The picture quality is fuzzy, but at least it's something. One day an old Three Stooges short comes on. The plot is dumb, but the slapstick is funny. At the end, the Three Stooges get in a car and zoom away.

Luis says, "Those cars can't go that fast."

Dallas says, "How would you know?"

With confidence, Luis says, "Because I've driven that kind of car before. They take forever to get up to twenty-five miles an hour and backfire constantly."

I ask, "When did you drive one of those?"

"When I was twelve. My family has owned and operated the same mechanic shop for five generations. My grandfather kept several antique cars and he let me drive one."

I didn't know that. I've been through so much with Luis, and I barely know him.

That night I finally asked Luis, "How did you end up in juvy?"

He shrugs. "I already told you back in basic. I got busted stealing a car."

There's more to it, I can feel it. "Don't give me the basic bitch answer. We've been through too much together and barely know each other. Come on."

My words hit him hard. He looks past me, at a time that was so long ago. "My family has owned and operated the same auto-shop for five generations. Growing up, I learned the ins and outs of every vehicle that came through. I could take apart an engine and put it back together by the time I was ten. I also learned how to start cars without the keys. I used that knowledge to look cool in high school. Unfortunately, I got the attention of some unsavory characters."

I stop him. "You don't have to sugar coat it."

He takes a deep breath. "Ok, fine. The gang convinced me to steal a fancy car. But while I was hot wiring it in the driveway, another gang member broke into the house and, while he was grabbing shit, the owner shot him. I was charged with felony murder because I was committing a felony while a known associate was murdered. I was looking at twenty-five to life when I was sixteen. When the war started and the military offered to clean my slate in exchange for service, of course I took it." He kind of smiles a bit. "I was scared shitless when I first got to juvy. That was when I met Angel. He had been in and out twice by that point, busted for possession with intent to sell. He showed me the ropes in juvy. He protected me from the more aggressive kids. He always had my back. He had no reason to, but that's just the kind of person he was. He even brought me into his gang for extra protection."

I see a small greenish tattoo on the inside of his bicep, but I can't make it out too well.

He starts to tear up a bit. "Angel was just a good goddamn person. He deserved better than what he got." He fights back the tears with anger. "It was all his dad's fault. He used Angel as a courier to sell drugs, to protect himself. The only time he visited Angel was to yell at him about how worthless he was for getting caught. Piece of shit." He can't fight back the tears anymore, and they burst from his eyes.

I hobble as best I can over to his bed and place my good hand on his shoulder, same as Angel did for me in Egypt. "I miss him too. He tried so hard to cheer me up when Rick died. I was trapped deep in my own head, and if he hadn't invited me to play cards with you guys, I probably would have killed myself." Was that true? I *was* in a very dark place after Rick died. Did that simple action of inviting me to play cards bring me back just enough to want to live again? Yeah, I think it did. It was just enough to remind me I still had friends around me. I miss all those I've lost, but I still have Luis.

Luis interrupts my inner monologue. "That's my story. What about you? I'm spilling my guts, but I don't know much about you either."

"There really isn't much. My parents work in a corporate office in Yuma. My mom is an engineer, and my dad is in sales. I have an older sister in college and an older brother in law school. I didn't have the grades for a university scholarship like my siblings. My mother really didn't want me to ever be associated with the military because her father came back a drunk and her brother died in Vietnam. But I think deep down I wanted to be drafted. I was just too afraid to admit it. I wanted the adventure of being part of something like this. Then maybe I could have some real stories to share. But after Rick died, all I wanted was to go home. There's no adventure here. Just bullshit and death."

Luis replies, "Bullshit and death."

I go back to my bed. "Maybe our adventure is finally over."

Maybe.

I didn't sleep much that night. I stare at the wall and think about life after this war. I'll go home, find a girl, get married, and have kids. Maybe I can find some kind of manual labor job and build a life. How can I love someone after all this? How could anyone love me for what I've become? Should I even go home? This place sucks, but it's simple. Follow orders and try not to die. Everything is provided for me. I don't know how to apply for a job. There's so much that wasn't taught to me in school and before I could get any kind of normal life experience, I was drafted. I don't really know how the world works outside of school or the army. I've never even had a girlfriend. I was too nervous to ever try in high school. Back home sounds too complicated. Maybe this is my place now.

CHAPTER 16

OVER A MONTH LATER AND my wounds have closed, I start physical therapy. I squeeze rubber balls to strengthen my left hand and work on my shoulder movement. Everything feels stiff. If I move my arm too high there is a slight pop and I get a jolt of pain. I'm lucky the bayonet didn't puncture a lung. It will take time to get my arm back. I prefer to use a crutch, but I can move without it.

Luis has to get an additional surgery to have shrapnel removed. The metal bits are dangerously close to his organs. He took the brunt of the explosion to his front and is still hiding his damage from me. I think he just wants to put on a brave face.

While Luis gets prepped for surgery, we watch the news showing clips from battles in other parts of the world.

Phil yells, "Look, there they are! They're in our atmosphere! The aliens are here!"

"Dude, calm down. It's just a plane."

Phil points to the corner of the screen. "No! It's them! I told you! They are here! Back me up, Gabe."

Gabe shrugs his shoulders, still unable to talk.

"I'm right! Aliens are here!" He starts shouting down the halls.

Orderlies have to restrain and drug him to calm him down. I think Phil should be transferred to the psych ward.

I need to be in this room less. With new mobility, I wander about the hospital. I've been stuck in that room for too long listening to Phil talk about aliens. I go outside to get some fresh air. It's winter and even this desert is cold. I take a deep breath of fresh air, which is full of cigarette smoke. The courtyard is full of wounded soldiers shivering as they smoke cheap cigarettes and try to calm themselves. An intense need hits me. I need to smoke. It has been too long. Too long in that bed, too long in pain, and too long without relief.

I approach a group of smokers huddled together. "Anyone have a spare cigarette?"

They ignore me, not wanting to give up precious smoke.

I try the next group, a slightly smaller crowd. Three standing with injuries to the arms, two of them amputees, then two in wheelchairs, one missing his legs. I say, "Can anyone spare cigarette?"

One glares at me from a wheelchair. "Who you with?" He's got one leg cut off above the knee and one cut off at the shin.

Who am I with? "What do you mean?"

He takes a short drag from his cigarette, then blows the smoke at me. It smells so intoxicating. He says, "Which branch did you serve?"

Oh, now I get it. Stick to your military branch. The last group was made out of very buff individuals, meaning they went through additional training, possibly Special Forces.

They won't want to deal with a scrub like me. While these guys look to be in my age group and relatively thin, I'll bet they're all half-starved army grunts like myself.

I say, "Army Infantry and drafted, if that makes a difference."

He nodded. "Same."

They make an opening for me and offer a cigarette.

I light it, sucking the harsh taste into my lungs. I feel lightheaded and calm a bit. "Thank you. I've been dying for a smoke."

The one in the wheelchair says, "You're welcome. The name's Maverick, but only one is free. These ain't cheap. They hike up the price at the store. They say it's a deterrent because they're bad for us. I don't see how it's any worse than the front lines. The smokes won't kill me for another forty years."

I hadn't thought about money very much. I have a salary of fifteen thousand, plus a hundred fifty weekly bonus for being in a combat zone. I've been here for at least six months, give or take. I'll have over eighteen grand when I get home. I've never had that much money before.

Maverick says, "I know that look. You're thinking about money, aren't you?"

How did he know?

"Well, don't get too excited. You'll have some cash, but they will take a lot of it for your current injury. As well as taxation for the war effort. Things ain't how they used to be. See, they passed a bunch of bills while we were fighting and dying." He pats his leg stump. "This is my second time here. First one was a hit to my bicep." He flexes his right arm, showing the scar. "That's when I found out that I had to pay out of pocket for my damages, which they took out of my account without telling me. Only found out because my wife and I share an account. They got away with it because this is a global war with the free world on the line. So, they cut corners on soldier's pay significantly to finance the war effort." He uses his hands to add literal quotes for this last part. "We're just meat for a grinder. To be used up and tossed aside."

I say, "What the fuck?!" I want to kick something, but my leg hurts too much. "Then why pay us at all?"

Maverick puts out his cigarette. "Because you still have to give us something for our sacrifice. The politicians like to talk about glory, but honestly, how much glory have you seen out there?"

An easy answer. "None." Just violence.

He lights a new cigarette. "Exactly! This is just a fuckin' war to clean the slate. Eliminate the lower levels of society, better known as us." He gestures to everyone in the group, each nodding in agreement. "So those in charge can restart everything, leaving us to die as the deserving poor. Those of us broken by the war are nothing to them. Just a burden they will find a way to dispose of us. Just watch."

This feels like the monologue of a super villain. I bet he's just exaggerating, or at least I hope. I'm sure I have plenty of money from this. More than enough to buy cigarettes. I remember Angel mentioning the same thing about the clean slate. It's all speculation without any proof.

I finish my smoke and say, "Thanks for the cigarette. I'm going to go buy more." An excuse to leave before I get pulled in any more.

They charge twenty bucks for a pack of cigarettes here. Fucking thieves! Plus, an additional five dollars for a cheap plastic lighter.

CHAPTER 17

DURING THE EARLY DAYS OF being able to walk, I wander to the psych ward. No one is guarding the door, so I go in out of pure curiosity. All the patient rooms have windows. I look into the first one. It's a tiny room with a man my age huddled in a corner, chewing on his thumb. All his fingertips are wrapped in bandages. He's crying without blinking and mumbling, "I didn't want it, I didn't want it, I didn't want it," over and over again.

I should not have come here.

An orderly sees me. "Hey! You shouldn't be here!"

"I was just leaving."

He pushes me out. He smells like cigarettes.

I hate how much that makes me want to smoke. I have to know even though I shouldn't ask. "What happened to that guy?"

The orderly looks back to where I gestured and sighs. "It's a damn shame. That kid was raped by his superior officer. He keeps chewing off his fingernails no matter what we do. Worst of all, I think that officer still has his rank. The higher-ups don't want it to go public, but fuck 'em. Now get out of here." The door closes.

I shouldn't have gone there.

While passing the gym, I think I see someone I know. "Hercules?" I limp back.

Sitting on a bench, curling a set of dumbbells is the Greek god of strength himself. "Forty-seven." He lifts the other arm. "Forty-eight." His veins are bulging. "Forty-nine." His arms tremble. "Fifty!" he exclaims and drops the weights to the ground with a thud. The imprint on them reads 70lb.

"Hercules!"

He spins around, meeting my eyes. He's as buff as ever, but his legs are gone. Just short lumps wrapped in bandages.

"Jason?" His face lights up with a huge smile. He uses his massive arms to lift himself off the bench and into a wheelchair, then rolls over to me. He hugs me so tight I fear he might break my ribs. "I'm so happy to see you!" He releases me.

I don't know what to say, then stumble through my words. "W-what happened?"

He looks down. "Got hit by an RPG in Kazakhstan." He then beats his chest in triumph. "But still got my dick." He jabs me lightly in the gut. "What about you?"

I look at my hand. I was really lucky. "I got stabbed by three different bayonets."

He looks shocked. "Were you at the Bayonet Battle of Baghdad?"

Cool name.

He goes on, "I heard the Chinese ran out of ammo and

did a bayonet charge as a last resort. You were one of the survivors?"

Other people know more about it than me. "Yeah, and Luis survived it too."

His smile grows even wider. "Really! Luis too? Is he here?"

"Yeah, he had an additional surgery yesterday. He's probably back in the room."

He starts to wheel himself out of the gym. "Well, let's go find him!"

I have to limp in a desperate attempt to catch him.

Luis is watching TV in our room, looking bored, until he sees the great Hercules burst through the door in a wheelchair.

His arms in the air, he announces himself, "Fear not, the great Hercules is here!"

We swap war stories. We liven up the tone to hide the pain of loss, but it's still there. Hercules tells us about Ranger School and his deployment. He had been dropped behind enemy lines in Kazakhstan when an RPG hit him. The explosion tore apart his legs. His staff sergeant, Barry Kane, saved him and carried him to the evac.

"Sergeant Kane always spoke about his great family line. To be born a Kane is to be born a killer. He was the greatest man I ever knew."

Kane. That name sounds familiar. "I knew a Kane back in middle school. I think his name was Austin Kane. He always said the same thing. To be born a Kane is to be born a killer."

"They were probably related. Sergeant Kane said he had a large family. And that each one of them is destined to kill."

To be born a Kane is to be born a killer. That is one hell of a fucked up family motto.

CHAPTER 18

SEVERAL MONTHS PASS, AND I'VE been able to exorcise regularly. I feel strong again. Hercules was shipped home. My physical therapy is going well. I turned nineteen and my tour should be coming to an end soon. I'd say about a month or so left. I feel good for the first time in a long time. Soon I'll be home and can start my life. Even if I don't know how to.

Our hospital roommates change as Gabe and Dallas have been medically discharged and sent back to the states. They say the Atlantic Ocean is the safest to cross, but I don't trust the military's version of safe. New occupants have taken their beds, both kids from our old company, no less. Kurt and Bob. I've never actually met someone named Bob before. Feels like an old name. They tell us how the platoon is doing. Apparently, Meatball has been promoted to lieutenant. I'll believe that when I see it, but I hopefully won't have too. They were injured by some kind of new drones and never saw any Chinese infantry while deployed. Instead, a swarm of bird-sized drones with helicopter blades flew in and cut them to ribbons.

Phil tells these kids about the upcoming alien invasion. I don't know why he's still here. He only lost one eye. Best guess. when he lost his eye, he also lost part of his brain. He went absolutely crazy when the news reported about an air battle in Ukraine. There was a picture of a blurry jet that Phil swore was an alien spacecraft. Nurses had to restrain him and knock him out with drugs. Luis and I had seen this happen before and weren't fazed, but the new kids were absolutely horrified. So goes another day in the infirmary.

Eventually, a doctor clears Luis and I to meet Colonel Salois, the officer in charge of this hospital. No one really told us anything about him. He's a recluse by all accounts and everyone who's met him soon disappears. My guess is they get sent home. God, I hope I'm right.

Colonel Salois's assistant has us check in first. I'm not sure if she's actually hot or I've just been without contact of the opposite sex for too long. I stare at her chest the entire time. Luis has to jab me to get me focused. I feel embarrassed, but she just smiles and winks.

Colonel Salois's office is absolutely massive, with a great third story view overlooking the nearby city. The ceiling is at least three times taller than me. One wall is decorated with a large portrait of him surrounded by fancy bookshelves with nothing but classic books, *Moby Dick*, *The Great Gatsby*, *Hamlet*. The other side has rows of file cabinets painted gold. In fact, the entire room gives off a yellow glow of gold. There is a large desk that would make any dictator jealous. Then I see a blond man with a short blond mustache. His hair is so blond it almost looks gold. He looks up from some files, his head resting on his hand.

Wait a second. That's the exact same pose in his portrait on the wall. I have to fight my smile as I stand at attention.

He says, "Private Jason Baker and Private Luis Martinez. I've been reading over your files. Looks like you've been through quite a lot. You were first deployed to Cairo, until it was bombed with chemical weapons. Then you were sent to Turkey until the invasion of Alaska required you elsewhere. Then you fought in the Battle for Baghdad, where you were both wounded. Is that correct?" He said that with no enthusiasm whatsoever.

We both reply, "Yes, sir."

He continues, "Good," and signs a document in each file and turns the page. "Alright, the doctors have deemed you both fit for service. Is that correct?"

I say, "To my knowledge, they have."

"A simple yes will suffice, Private Baker."

"Yes, sir."

He signs the document and turns the page. "It appears that both of you have earned accommodations for your service. You'll both be awarded a Purple Heart for being wounded in the call of duty. You will both receive a Combat Infantry Badge for fighting in active ground combat while members of an infantry unit. Finally, you will both be awarded the Bronze Star Medal for your heroic actions during the Bayonet Battle of Baghdad, where Beta Company held off a charging enemy with bayonets, which led to our eventual victory and control of Baghdad." He puts the least amount of enthusiasm into this announcement as possible, then takes out two small boxes of medals, pushes them forward on the desk, and signs the document.

He turns the page. "It appears that both of you have

been promoted to squad leaders as well. This came from the commanding officer of Beta Company, Major Hugo, after the Battle of Baghdad." He takes out two staff sergeant patches. "Attach those before reporting back to your unit."

I always thought getting medals would be a grander experience. That's what they show on TV, but instead, I get an uninterested colonel reading about one of the worst days of my life.

"Very good. Both of you will return to your Beta Company of the Second Infantry Battalion, where you, Sergeant Baker, will serve the remaining ninety-five days of your tour. Please sign the bottom of these documents, take your medals, and talk to my assistant Vicki. She has the details for returning to your battalion."

Wait, ninety-five days? I thought I only had a month left. Did I miscount? When did I get sent to Egypt? I know I lost count while I was in Turkey. Shit, that's *so* much time left.

Vicki is very nice and congratulates us on our medals, then explains the fine details about our departure. She gives us paperwork for new uniforms. Unfortunately, all our gear that we had back in Baghdad was lost when we were sent here. That means my spare TP and brand new socks are gone. She does give us some mail we had missed, and I anxious to get a chance to read it.

Vicki winks at us on the way out.

Luis says, "I'm going to miss her."

"Yeah, she was pretty."

He nudges me. "No, I'm going to *miss* her."

Why did he emphasize the miss? Then it clicks. "You had sex with her? When? And how?"

He holds up his hands to visually demonstrate. "We'll you put your dick in the vagina to have sex."

"Not what I mean, you jackass. How the hell did you hook up with a woman that beautiful?"

He smiles. "Oh, you didn't know? For the right price, she will give you the best night of your life."

"Why didn't you tell me about that? You know I'm a virgin."

He shrugs. "Must have slipped my mind."

"No, you just wanted her for yourself, didn't you?"

He doesn't answer.

"So that's where you kept disappearing to. How much money did you end up spending anyway?"

He doesn't answer.

"You spent everything you had, didn't you?"

He answers, "Yeah, but it was worth it."

I can't blame him. She is very beautiful. I doubt I even have enough money for her anyway. I spent so much money on cigarettes.

We have to catch a ride in a truck to an airfield to fly back into the war zone. Then we take another truck to a helicopter that takes us to a forward operating base and then take a smaller truck to Beta Company.

On the plane, I read letters from my parents. They love me very much and wish me a speedy recovery. I really should write them back and let them know I've recovered. I have a letter from my brother Pete too. He hopes I'm kicking ass and winning this war single-handedly. I don't know how to respond to that. I can't tell him the truth. He won't understand. The other letter I thought was lost long ago. It's from Alex, a dead man's letter. I don't know if I can read it.

Luis asks, "Are you going to read it?"

I didn't realize I was shaking. "I…I don't know. This is from my high school friend. He died months ago on a naval ship when Russia invaded Alaska. This is the last thing I will ever have of him. I don't know if I *can* read it."

Luis says, "You should. It's your last chance to hear his words." I take a deep breath and open it.

Dear Jason,

I know you're in a dark place right now. We all are. Rick was a good friend, and we miss him dearly. I want you to know we are still here and will always be with you. This war will be over before you know it and we can all mourn him together.

Your friend always, Alex

Goddamn, I miss them so much. Just like that, all the pain I had buried comes flooding back out and I cry. This shouldn't have happened. We should be at home enjoying life after high school, getting laid, and doing dumb things that make great stories later. But instead, they're all dead and it's just me now.

No! I force it all back down. I can't think of what-ifs. I have to think about surviving. I have to live to remember them. I'm the only one who can.

CHAPTER 19

BACK WITH BETA COMPANY, WE meet with our new CO, Lieutenant Meatball. I've got a bad feeling about this.

"Jason, Luis, welcome back! I hope your vacation was refreshing."

Luis responds, "Healing from stab wounds and shrapnel is truly a relaxing vacation."

Easy on the sarcasm, dude. Not to mention, you actually got laid.

Meatball continues, ignoring Luis's response, "Well, while you two were relaxing, you missed the fight against Iraq. Now we're almost through Afghanistan, then we'll hit the chinks in their homeland. I see you are also my new sergeants. Now I know we're friends from basic, but it is important to not undermine my authority. It would demoralize the rest of the platoon. Understand?"

Luis and I both agree but with as little enthusiasm as we can. I don't want to be in charge, but I don't want to leave everyone's survival to Meatball either.

The rest of the platoon look like pissed off kids. There's

no one left from Baghdad. Just a bunch of new kids. There are two separate groups playing cards. One in the middle of the tent and one in the corner. The one in the corner is a more diverse group than the rest of the troops.

Luis nodes his head to the diverse group. "See those kids?"

I nod.

"See how their tattoos have a green tint? Those are prison tats. The ink used in the joint is low quality and turns green once in the skin."

I did not know that. "Looks like there's some divide. You talk to the prison kids, and I'll find out how long the others have been here."

Luis sits down with the former delinquents, who tense up, but he shows them a tattoo on his forearm and they relax.

I go up to the other group. "Care to deal another in?"

They look at me.

I know I look like a new recruit, clean-shaven with a brand new uniform.

A short burly redhead says, "Sure, buy-in is pretty steep though. What do you have to wager?"

I pull out a pair of brand new socks I snagged on the way out of the hospital. They try to hide their lust, but I see it.

The burly redhead tries to hide his excitement. His thick southern accent shines through. "That will work. The game is Texas Hold 'em."

They deal me some cards.

One of them notices my hand still bandaged. "Stab yourself in basic?"

I hold up my hand. "No, I got stabbed a couple of times in Baghdad." Then I show them the scar in my shoulder. "I've been in the hospital, recovering. Unfortunately, they didn't let me keep the bayonets."

Their looks immediately change, now that they know I ain't no cherry.

The tallest one says, "I thought everyone except for the lieutenant was dead."

"No, but most are. Me and Luis over there have been off the line recovering, and I remember a bunch of troops ran. What happened to them?"

They all look at each other, then back to me.

The redhead says, "We heard about Baghdad from them. They got us through the Iranian invasion, but they're gone now. Fucking drones cut them to ribbons. The drones were hard to hit with a rifle. We had to start using shotguns with buckshot."

One with the start of a beard says between drags from a cigarette, "We ain't even seen a Chink yet, just fucking drones."

The tallest one says, "We did fight some of the Iranian troops, but the drones all but wiped them out."

The redhead continues, "And the lieutenant has been all but useless. Idiot can't tell his ass from a hole in the ground."

The smoker says, "And all we have to replace our losses are fucking delinquents."

This is worse than I thought. Robots as our opponents, Meatball is in charge, and two squads that don't want to work together. Three months might as well have been a year.

I look each man in the eyes as I say, "Listen, the lieutenant may not be the best leader, but I'm your new sergeant and we will need to work together if we want to make it out of this. For starters, call me Jason. What are your names?"

"The tall one is Michael. The one with the cigarette wants to be called Grimes," the redhead says. "I'm James, and the quiet one is Lee."

I hadn't even noticed the pale kid sitting on the ground with a thousand-yard stare.

Luis and I exchange notes about the squads. "The future of warfare is now. We'll be fighting drones for the foreseeable future."

Luis says, "The delinquents said the same fuckin' thing. We'll need to get shotguns with bird shot or buck. What's the difference between them?"

I actually know the answer. "Bird shot is smaller, used for hunting pigeons so they don't explode when you hit them. Buck is better for fighting people at close range." I only know that from Uncle Steve, when I went shooting as a kid.

Luis says, "We'll have to see the supply officer, whoever that is now. The delinquents are going to be tough to work with. They do not like authority."

I say, "There is a split in the platoon."

Luis says, "We'll have to figure it out. We all have to survive Meatball's leadership."

I ask, "How long are their deployments?"

Luis answers, "They were given the opportunity to enlist same as I was, in exchange for their sentences, so four to eight years."

What? That's so long. "Eight years? I thought it was only four."

Luis says, "It's all in the wording, but they can keep you

for eight if they need you. Angel pointed that out to me. They're bitter because they thought this would be easier than prison, or at least a better option. Now they don't think they will be going home."

CHAPTER 20

T HE SMALL MOUNTAIN TOWN IS deserted. Just empty buildings and old corpses. Based on the decay, I would guess the civilians were killed two weeks ago. The platoon checks every building for possible survivors, but there's nothing here. Whoever came through here took everything.

"Incoming drones!"

Swarms of hawk sized machines descend from a low flying plane. Their three propeller blades buzz like tiny helicopters.

We open fire with assault rifles, hoping to take them out before they get any closer. We don't. Each drone holds thirty rounds of armor piercing bullets, then depending on their range to a target, they self-destruct.

I switch to my secondary weapon, a cheap pump-action hunting shotgun. Thankfully, the drones are made out of cheap plastic to improve mobility. Thank God I didn't need special permission to bring a civilian weapon into combat, but I'm still pissed that I had to order it myself because the army can't afford to supply an entire platoon with extra weapons and bird shot. So, everyone bought what they could. It's not like there's much else we can spend our hard earned paychecks on.

Michael was too close to a drone after it ran out of ammo. The blast left a cavern where his face used to be. There was nothing I could do, yet I am responsible for him. I shouldn't be leading them, and neither should Meatball. He only cares about glory. He always volunteers our platoon to take point, but then he's never in front. He chews me out for failing my men, but he's just mad that the large troop losses reflect poorly on him. However, that doesn't stop him from volunteering us for the most dangerous missions again, and the cycle continues.

Michael's replacement gets killed almost immediately as well as that quiet kid, Lee, and three from Luis's team. The third squad gets completely wiped out. I decide to not bother with names anymore, because they all die so quickly. We're always short on men, but Meatball still volunteers us to be in front. Throw enough shit at a target and eventually you'll hit something.

The current rumor is that the drones use facial recognition software to pick targets, which allows them to hunt for targets of higher value or someone who has been in several battles. But they killed a private instead of me, so I doubt the software is that good. Although he had been fighting the drones longer than I had.

"I put you in charge because I trusted you to lead these men, but you keep getting them killed. Do you not know how to lead?" Meatball doesn't let me respond and turns to Luis. "And I gave you the delinquent squad. As a delinquent yourself, you should be able to empathize with them, but you're just as useless."

I'm so sick of his shit. "First of all, you didn't promote us, the major did. Second, we were ambushed by a swarm of drones. The village was supposed to be under Russian control, so we didn't prepare our shotguns. We were screwed the second a swarm of Chinese drones came out of the sky. Maybe if you had waited for better intel before sending us in—"

Meatball screams, "Shut the fuck up!"

He wants another promotion, but we are not as good as Angel was.

Then Luis grabs Meatball's lapel and pushes him backward into a Humvee. "Mother fucker! You want glory so goddamn bad!" Luis winds up for a punch, but I grab his arm and shove myself in between them.

"Enough! We are not doing this!" I glare at Luis with as much bravado as I can muster.

Luis holds on for another second longer, then reluctantly lets go.

Meatball straightens his uniform and snorts at Luis, "Insubordination!" He glances at me. "At least someone knows his place."

I get right in his face. "Listen here, Meatball," I say shaking with rage., "I didn't do that for you. I did that for him." And I walk away. I need at least one person I can rely on in this shit storm.

We make camp in the ruins of a village that was destroyed weeks ago. We have to maintain darkness, so no fires and no uncovered lights. Meatball gets to sleep in the only building with a roof. I have to talk to him about resupply and any other new info from the captain with first platoon five miles away in their own destroyed village. The door is just a blanket.

"Meatball, you in here?"

I hear muttering and clicking sounds, then go in and find Meatball cleaning his light machine gun, holding a flashlight in his mouth. "Lieutenant Meatball, what's the word on resupply?"

He keeps cleaning his gun but spits out the flashlight. "We'll get some supplies at the rendezvous with the rest of the company tomorrow." He starts putting his weapon back together. "We'll also be getting new orders as well." He turns to me and smiles a big toothy smile that doesn't put me at ease.

"Thank you. That's all I needed to know." I turn to leave, but something holds me there. "Meatball, why are you here?" I need to know why he joined the army. He acts like a spoiled brat and clearly has no idea what he's doing.

He stops smiling. "What do you mean, Sergeant?" He's clearly trying to make me feel inferior by bringing up rank.

"Why did you enlist? I'm here because I had no choice. Most of us didn't have much of a choice. But you come from a wealthy background, or at least that's what the general believes."

He finishes assembling his gun, cocks it, and pulls the trigger with a click. "I want to be great. I want to be a badass and prove to everyone that I'm not worthless. The army has given me that chance, and I will succeed no matter what. I'll show all those jerks back in school just how tough I am!" He stands up. He's a tad shorter than me, but his anger makes him seem bigger. "Everyone always doubted me, but I have become strong. Here I can do what I want and no one can stop me anymore."

I shake my head like I understand, but I just want to leave.

"Here I have become great! And everyone finally sees how great I am!"

I say, "Got it," then quickly make my exit.

I do understand the want to be great, but after everything he's done… I remember the civilian bodies in Baghdad. I think his view of being great is his kill count. He's a sick bastard. I bet fighting a robotic enemy is making him crazier. He needs to be kicked out, sent home. I need to do something, but what? I don't want to make things worse.

CHAPTER 21

I<small>T'S HOT AND WE'RE LOW</small> on both food and water. Supplies have been getting smaller with each resupply, and that's if we even get a resupply. We're fighting on too many fronts. Now we stand outside a small city that is supposed to be Russian controlled and we can't just bomb it because of small civilian presence. Several of us are at the point of saying, "Fuck it, just drop the bombs," but we don't make the call, so we have to do this the hard way.

My squad is still down two men and James was given command of squad three, but they're all new kids fresh from the world. Meatball volunteered us to take point again. Luis still looks pissed, and I'm worried about what he'll do.

As we load up for combat, I confront Luis. "Listen, I don't know what you're planning, but please don't do anything stupid."

He finishes loading his shotgun, cocking it angrily.

"I'm all for getting rid of him, but, Luis, if you kill him, you will be court-martialed and likely executed."

He clicks the safety on and slings the gun over his shoulder. "I ain't done shit, so quit your worrying."

"Listen, I don't like him anymore than you do, but when his number is up, it's up. I'm out of here in thirty days. I want to see you back home, not in a military prison."

Luis points to his head. "Open your eyes, Jason. Ain't none of us getting out of here. Have you heard of anyone actually making it to the end of their deployment in one piece?" He storms off to prepare his men.

Everyone before us is dead or missing pieces and no one from my graduation class is left either. I *can* get home in one piece. I have to hold onto that. Meatball enlisted, so he has four years of service even if he is incompetent. Luis has the same amount of time. I want out, to leave all of this behind me, but that will mean abandoning Luis to deal with Meatball alone. That will end badly.

More door to door fighting. At least it's something I'm good at. The Russians are fortified and we're low on manpower. I don't think we can win this. I fire two rounds into a door before kicking it down. I'm not fucking around. Sure enough, there's a dead Russian on the ground. The room has a cool tint from a stained glass window of blue and yellow. A grenade lands at the bottom of the staircase right next to me. Shit! I throw it back up. The explosion drops down dust. I don't hear anything, so I run up the stairs, finding another dead Russian and two dead civilians. Were they already dead? This is war. There are no right choices.

When I get back out, Luis is yelling, "Pull back!"

Oh god, what now? I see a swarm of drones descending. We can't fight both them and the Russians.

I start to run.

Meatball is distracted with shooting at the swarm. Five bullets pierce through his body, and he stands there for a second, looking at me. He can't process what just happened. Then the drone detonates and the explosion rips off half his face, throwing him to the ground.

I stand still, wanting to run away, but I can't.

"Medic!" I grab his limp body and drag him back into the building. "Medic!" No one is coming. Everyone has already retreated. On my radio, I yell, "Lieutenant down, need help! I'm in a brown building with yellow and blue windows."

No response.

A Russian trooper sees me, but I shoot first. Three rounds drop him. I had to shoot out part of the window to make the shot.

I try to stop Meatball's bleeding, but there are too many wounds. The chest wounds punched through his lungs, and he's barely breathing. I have to get him out, but he's too big to carry alone, easily twice my weight.

Bullets zing past. I'm too close to a fight with two enemy forces. I'll die if I stay, and I'll die if I try to move him. I should have left him. This was a mistake. But I just can't abandon him. Meatball may be an unbearable asshole, but I won't just leave someone to die, not when I can do something. I refuse to be that dead inside.

Out of the dust, the scraggly private with a lit cigarette in his mouth says, "Sergeant Jason!"

I wave. "Grimes, I am so happy to see you. Over here!"

He runs as fast as he can through the chaos all around him. We can carry Meatball out together. I feel a small sliver of hope until a large round takes off Grime's foot. He falls, sliding to a stop and holding his leg. Shit! I look at Meatball, my commanding officer, one of the few left from basic. His eyes have rolled back into his head. I think he's still breathing, but it's too faint to tell. I have to make a call. Grimes still has a chance. He's one of my men, my responsibility.

"I'm sorry, Meatball." I run as fast as I can, firing blindly in the hopes of creating some kind of cover and then sliding next to Grimes as bullets zing past me. I feel my arm get struck by something hard, but I can't let it stop me. Grimes grabs hold of me as I lift him on my shoulders. He still has fight left in him. I run with everything I have left. Grimes screams every cuss word he knows as he lays down suppressive fire.

We rendezvous into the rest of the company just outside town. The new medic quickly begins to treat Grimes's leg.

"God fucking damn it! Those mother fucking commies took my foot! I hope you fuckers choke on it and die!" Grimes never stops cursing as he's taken away for evac.

My arm got grazed on the way out, but not enough for me to go with Grimes.

Captain Hill asks where the lieutenant is.

"He didn't make it, sir. Drones got him. I had to get Grimes out."

He looks at me like he knows exactly what happened. "You did what you could." He turns to the rest of the company. "That's everyone. Mount up."

Luis asks, "What about the town, sir?"

"Marines are on the way to finish the fight. They will retrieve the lieutenant's body. Our work here is done."

I watch the flickering lights as the trucks leave. With the sun setting, it almost looks beautiful. Almost. What was the point of that? No victory, only loss. Luis doesn't say anything. No good riddance or cheers of joy. Just silence. Meatball's body will be discovered eventually. There was nothing more I could have done, but I don't know if I believe that. There are no right choices in war.

CHAPTER 22

THREE DAYS LEFT UNTIL I get to go home. I'm ready to leave. This place has given me too many scares. My left hand is still stiff. I never did get a chance to write to Mom and Dad, but I'll see them soon enough. Fuck this place. Fuck this war.

Luis and his squad almost threw a party when they heard about Meatball. It all feels wrong. Maybe I should have just left him in the street, then Grimes wouldn't have been injured. We'll likely get a kid fresh from the world to be our lieutenant, who thinks he can lead us despite never having been in combat.

We're ordered to clean up while we're off the line awaiting replacements for all the troops we've lost. The army set up some rudimentary tent showers for us. I haven't showered in months and had sand in a lot of uncomfortable places. The water is cold, but I'll take what I can get. We also have to shave, but we don't have any shaving cream. Ended up cutting my face a bunch. My face looks so old, though I'm only nineteen.

One of the base's many runners barges in. "Sergeant Jason Baker, Captain Hill wants to see you!"

This could be it! Not enough time to send me on a new mission. I'm going home! "Understood. I'm on my way."

I have to turn off my smile when I get to Captain Hill's barracks. His place is nice. It actually has a cot with a sleeping bag and a real pillow. I've been using my helmet this whole time. I'll probably need to see a chiropractor when I get home.

Smiling, Captain Hill says, "I have good news for you, Sergeant."

Oh boy! Here it comes!

"I'm promoting you to second lieutenant." He hands me a lieutenant bar.

"Wait, what?" Shit, I said that out loud.

Still smiling, Captain Hill continues, "Surprising, I know. You're now a commissioned officer. It's rather unheard of for a draftee to receive such an honor, but you have proven time and again with your heroics that you deserve this. It was the major's decision, and I know you won't let us down."

Wait, I haven't been heroic at all. I've done what I had to survive my tour, which is almost over! I've only done what I had to do. What anyone would do. I am not special enough for this. He's just smiling at me, reveling in my shock. I force my internal screaming to stop.

"Sir, with all due respect, my tour ends in three days. Promoting me seems…" How can I say this nicely? "It seems unnecessary."

His smile leaves his face. "You haven't heard the news?"

I say, "I haven't heard much of anything, sir. We've been on the move so much that my knowledge outside of our current mission has been nothing but rumors that I've done my best to ignore."

He sighs. "Troop demands have been mounting up, so congress passed a bill that extended the draft tour from one year of service to two."

What! Are you kidding me! No! You can't do this to me!

The captain continues, "I'm sorry you had to find out this way. You're being promoted because we won't be getting a replacement for your friend, Lieutenant Melvin, or Meatball as everyone called him, and I need someone with a clean background and battlefield experience." He pushes the lieutenant bar into my hand. "I know you won't disappoint." Then he turns to a map and begins explaining the next mission.

I leave his barracks, go behind the fueling station for the vehicles where it's always loud, and scream from the bottom of what's left of my heart, "Fuck!" I punch an empty truck. I gave them a year of my life. I punch the truck again. I've given them my blood. I punch it harder. All my friends are dead, but they still want more. I drop to my knees. What more do I even have?

Sitting here isn't going to fix a goddamn thing. I stand up and put on a glove to hide my swollen knuckles. It's now my job to unite everyone. I can now do what Meatball never could.

I go into my platoon's tent where a bunch of fresh-faced kids are trying to mingle with the vets. I announce with a bit more bass in my voice than normal, "Second platoon!"

All of the cherries jump to attention while all the vets stay seated, rolling their eyes.

With confidence that I didn't know have, I say, "I have

been promoted to lieutenant as Meatball's replacement. I promise that I will strive to do better than my predecessor. I have been informed of our new mission. We will be leading an assault on the city of Kunduz. It has been the primary location for production of drones for the Chinese in Afghanistan. We believe that the Chinese are pulling out of Afghanistan. Our mission is to liberate the civilian population that has been enslaved for production. Russian forces are believed to be advancing on Kunduz as well. However, we do not have a time frame for them yet. Be prepared for drone fighting as well as troop fighting in door-to-door combat."

Should I tell them about the draft being extended?

I swallow hard. I'm not going to bullshit them. "Also, for those who were drafted, if you have not heard already, the tour has been extended to two years instead of one."

I hear a few vets curse loudly.

"We leave in one hour."

Luis catches me. "I told you, ain't none of us getting out of this alive."

I say, "Thanks for the encouragement, asshole."

He elbows me in the gut. "Just don't get me killed."

"I promise to try."

We convoy to Kunduz, with choppers close behind. My Humvee is full of nothing but cherries. They look so young. I bet they've never even shaved. I turn to the one sitting closest to me. "How old are you, Private?"

He says, "I'm seventeen, sir."

Sweet Christ! I say, "Why the hell are you here? You're just a kid." Realizing full well I'm only two years older, I still can't imagine why anyone would want this so soon.

He says, "It's a family thing, sir. My dad let me sign up right after I graduated high school. But I'm ready for this. I've been looking forward to this my entire life. I'm ready to kill some commies."

The driver nods in agreement and the gunner yells, "Hell yeah!"

I shake my head and say, "Don't worry. This fight will pop your cherries real quick. It's not all it's cracked up to be."

The kid says, "Well, I ain't scared. You see, my family has a motto that has been passed down for centuries."

Why does this sound familiar?

"To be born a Kane is to be born a killer. And I am ready to kill, sir."

Great, he's a psycho from a family of psychos.

Wait a damn second! "Austin Kane?"

The kid says, "That's me."

"I went to middle school with you. We had Social Studies together. How are you two years younger than me?"

Kane says, "My family moved around a lot when I was a kid. I ended up in the wrong grade more than once."

CHAPTER 23

THERE'S A SMELL OF SMOKE in the air in the empty city. All the buildings are untouched. I don't like this. It feels like a ghost town. Over the radio, I say, "We don't see anything from the ground. What's the view from above? Over."

Static, then, "There appears to be a burned down building two klicks to your west. Possibly the warehouse for drone manufacturing. Proceed with caution. Over."

"Roger. Proceeding to the wreckage."

The convoy turns west, and the smell gets stronger. The building has been reduced to rubble and has the unmistakable smell of burned, rotting flesh.

One of the cherries asks, "What is that smell?"

I say, "It's burnt shit. Everyone shits when they die. You'll get used to it."

The Chinese locked all the native workers inside the warehouse before setting it on fire.

Kane says, "This is dishonorable. How could they do this?"

I laugh. "Ha! Dishonorable? This is *war*. There's no

honor in war. Hell, I appreciate how efficiently they did this. Now we know exactly where production of drones was and that it's destroyed. We don't have to search the entire city. Plus, cleanup is all in one spot. You should have seen Cairo after the dirty bomb. Corpses were everywhere. It was a huge pain in the ass to clean up." I'm being too cynical with the new kids, but I can't help it. This is common stuff in war that they need to get used to.

Over the radio, "Lieutenant Baker, do you copy? Over."

"I'm here. Over."

Captain Hill orders, "Take your platoon to secure the capitol building at the center of town."

Beats doing the cleanup. "Roger that. Over."

There's nothing left. All the cars have been drained of fuel. There's no food and all water sources have been contaminated with corpses. They didn't want to leave anything behind. At least all the buildings are still standing. It's easy to form a perimeter in a ghost town. The capitol building looks new. I would guess it was built in the last five years or so. Probably built by the US military during its occupation, before this war started. I'm surprised the Chinese didn't burn it down.

We get set to clear the building. "Luis, take your squad through the first floor. I'll take First Squad through the second floor. Squad Three, hold the perimeter."

Luis jabs my shoulder. "You're already doing better than Meatball."

"We just started. You have to give me time to fuck up."

Then the radio shouts, "Planes! Incoming!"

The sky erupts with sounds of jets breaking the sound

barrier. I know that sound all too well. It's the Russians. They want this city for the same reason we do.

I start barking orders. "Find cover!"

Got to get in the building. There's an explosion at the warehouse as fire erupts into the sky. Then missiles hit the convoy, and the explosion throws me into the building. Everything goes dark as I hit the ground.

My head is throbbing, and I taste blood. The world is blurry but slowly comes back into focus. My ears ring with pain. I can't hear anything else. I feel my chest, stomach, and crotch. Everything is still there. The blood in my mouth is from biting my tongue, so it could be worse.

I try to stand, but I'm stuck. Oh, no. My left arm is stuck under the rubble. Shit, it's gone numb. That's not a good sign. I try to move some of the rubble, but it's too heavy for one arm. Is there anyone else here? "Help! Anyone there?"

Just rubble and body parts scattered everywhere. Blood oozes out from under the collapsed debris that used to be the front entrance. I'm on my own.

I take out my knife, shove it into a small gap in the rubble, and apply as much force as I can. "Come on." I can feel the blade bend. "Come on, mother fucker! Move!" There's a tiny release of pressure, and I yank my arm out.

My hand is mangled, and blood spurts from stumps that used to be fingers. The numb feeling leaves, and all I feel is pain. I shove my mangled hand into my opposite armpit, hoping to stop the bleeding, but I feel the blood drip down my side.

"Fucking shit!"

I make a quick tourniquet and wrap it as best I can with

one arm. I'm not dying here, god damn it. Focus, what do I need to do now?

Check for survivors and find a way out. This building is too unstable to stay here. I bet ground troops are engaging my left over men. I won't be much good in a fight. I need evac.

My hearing is coming back. "Sound off! Any survivors?"

Still nothing.

I try my radio, but there's a large piece of metal sticking out of it. Luckily, it didn't go all the way through.

I see a hand sticking out of the rubble. I move what I can and grab the hand. "I've got you!" I pull and it comes out easily with the forearm, but that's it. I try to dig deeper. There's nothing but severed body parts. My best guess it that there are enough body parts here to make up three people.

There are two smashed bodies on the floor, both from Luis's squad. I turn to the last body, seeing dog tags still around the neck. The vest protected that much, but most of the head was gone. The dog tags confirm my fear. It's Luis, my last friend. There wasn't anything I could have done. I can't cry now. I have to get out of here. I can hear muffled gunshots from outside.

Rest now, my friend. Your journey is over.

There has to be an exit out back. There's only one door out of the lobby and, of course, it's locked. I swear, "I will kill the idiot who locked this." I kick it as hard as I can, but it barely moves. "God damn it." I take a running start using my momentum to kick and fly through the door, landing on my face. It hurt my mangled hand more than my head.

What the hell is this room? Wires strung up to every wall and door all connect to a large object in the center of the room. It appears to be a missile with no propulsion system. It's making a humming sound. A mushroom cloud is drawn on the side and a clock is counting down from fifteen seconds.

"Oh my God…"

I drop to my knees. I've killed us all. They're going to nuke us. They left this at the center of the city for maximum damage. They couldn't fire a nuclear missile without immediate retaliation, but one planted in a city where three armies are fighting? The debate over who did what will keep everyone from retaliating. They even killed all the civilians to ensure a military member would be the one to open the door.

I don't know how to deactivate a nuclear bomb. I can't outrun the blast within ten seconds.

I'm sorry, Mom and Dad. I won't be coming home. Goodbye, Pete. Goodbye, Ann. I'll miss you two. I wish I could be home, but this is it. I'm sorry, Captain. I wasn't ready to lead after all. I'll tell you on the other side. My friends, Rick, Zack, Alex, Angel, Luis, and even Meatball, I'll see you guys real soon.

I feel no pain. There is only light. Time slows down, and every second feels like a lifetime. I can see every day I have ever lived, every school day, the good days with friends, and the bad days of war. Everything that shaped me into the man I was.

My life was short, but it was mine.

CHAPTER 24

THE WORLD SPINS AS I fall onto hard rubber ground. My head is pounding. Everything is so bright that it makes my eyes hurt. I keep blinking and rubbing them in a desperate attempt to bring my surroundings into focus. "Where am I?"

Slowly the light fades. I'm in a gray seat made out of cheap leather.

A closer look at my surroundings reveals I'm in a long tube with small windows to two parallel rows of seats. In each gray seat is a kid between the age of twelve and fourteen. Their faces look familiar, but I can't place them. The tube feels like it's moving. Am I on a school bus?

The kid in the seat next to me says in a distorted voice, "Final approach, are you ready?"

I haven't fully collected myself. "Zack?" Why are you so young? I rub my eyes in disbelief. That's definitely Zack, even if he looks to be about twelve. He must be here to guide me to the other side. The vehicle stops and all the kids rush out. I grab my backpack and follow.

"What the actual fuck?" This isn't heaven. This is middle school.

A massive school monitor in an orange vest says, "Hey! Watch your language."

Fuck off, I think, but once I see our astronomical size difference, I decide to keep that one in my head.

This doesn't feel like the afterlife. I feel physically awkward and uncomfortable in my own body. This can't be heaven. Maybe it's hell. I did a lot of bad things in the war, but then, why isn't everything on fire and where are all the scary demons?

Zack walks through the school courtyard, weaving through the crowds of students. I run after him. He meets up with a group of three familiar faces. I stop dead in my tracks. It's Rick with his big blond afro and Alex who is so tall. Zack breaks into the conversation by literally jumping into the middle. I've missed them so much. And then there's Tommy, that kid who always hung around us because his mom is friends with Zack's mom. What the fuck is Tommy doing here? He's not dead. He was too unhealthy to get into the military.

I can't hear anyone speaking. Why the hell is my hearing still so distorted? I clean out my ear with my pinky and in an instant, the world becomes clear. But my pinky is dripping blood. That can't be good.

There is nothing I want more than to go be with my friends, but something isn't right. I need a private place to think. I turn to go inside the building. I can hide in the bathroom.

The massive monitor stops me, "You can't go in until the bell rings."

He might actually be a demon. I'm not ready for that kind of fight. "Come on, man. I gotta take a dump."

"Oh, go ahead." He waves me past.

What is your purpose, giant man?

The bathroom has broken tile. The stalls have dents, and there are carvings of profanity on every service. Just like it's always looked. It would be considered crappy, but after the war, this isn't too bad. I take the second farthest stall to the back corner because I remember the farthest one had a flimsy bolt lock. I drop my hundred pound backpack. How the hell did I carry that every day?

I can figure this out. If I'm dead, I won't be able to feel pain. Though my ear is bleeding and my nose is stuffy, which I blow into some toilet paper. Blood mixed with mucus comes out, but my sinuses are clear. Wow, this place smells terrible. Do the janitors ever clean this room? I look at my left hand. I remember it was mangled and I was missing most of my fingers. Yet right now, it's perfectly fine. No scars anywhere, not even a bruise. I have to shock myself back to the real world. I take out a paperclip from my backpack and unfold it into a point, then place it just under my left pinky finger. The pain from this should connect to the pain in the real world and pull me back. Just got to do it fast. I shove it deep under my nail, sending pain shooting up my arm.

"Damn it! Wake up! I'm not done yet." My hand's shake as blood begins to seep out. My heart races, my adrenaline spikes. "This is real, this is all real."

I pull out the paperclip. Was the war just a horrible dream I had on the way to school? No, I have memories of my life before the war. Memories of high school days still to come. I remember the last Christmas with my grandparents before they passed away in 2010. I even remember the next presidential election in 2008. I remember watching *South Park* joke about having a black president. I remember all that perfectly. Each of those days happened, or at least will happen.

I need to collect myself. I wrap my bloody pinky in toilet paper. Ok, what happened right before the light that brought me here? I was in a room with a nuclear bomb. Is this divine intervention? No, there has to be more logic behind going back in time and there is no god. The war proved that to me. The bomb must have sent me back.

The bell rings.

Oh shit. I have to get to class. Wait, what class do I have?

I have ten minutes to figure this out and start digging through my backpack. In middle school, I was issued a planner to keep track of my classes. Found it. Let's see, 2007 is imprinted across the cover. The current page is marked with a paperclip. Monday October 23 has assignments written under it. So today is Tuesday the 24th. I'm in 6th grade, and if the assignments are in order, then my first class is math. I think it was off an odd corner across from my locker. Oh shit. I have a locker. Please tell me I still have the locker combo written down. It's close enough to the beginning of the year, so I might still have it. Bingo! Hidden deep in my pack, locker 151 combination 15-0-5.

I count the locker numbers to find mine, and just around the corner is my math class. I should know the way better. I walked this path a thousand times as a kid. It was so long ago but feels like only yesterday. We weren't allowed to carry our backpacks around school for security reasons, something to do with gang violence, so I take out my massive binder and my math book. I think that was the only class I had to carry my textbook to. Christ, it's heavy. How weak am I? I didn't do sports until high school, and I didn't start lifting weights until I hit puberty.

Oh great, I have to go through puberty again.

I actually went back in time. This is amazing. I stop just before I reach my class as I realize what that truly means. I have knowledge of what is to happen and can avoid all the bad stuff. Or I could make things worse. But I do have a wealth of experiences that none of these kids has. Mostly bad experiences, but now I can avoid those. Fuck, that's so confusing it makes my head hurt. I have had bad experiences that made me tougher, but now I can avoid those situations, but then would I still have the knowledge that shaped me from the bad experiences?

I can think about the paradox later.

I enter my math class, betting the rest will be like riding a bike. Now where do I sit? Oh no… All my classes had assigned seating. I don't remember any of them. The teacher is writing some equations on the board. I can ask her, but I don't remember her name. "Excuse me…where do I sit?"

She doesn't turn around. "In your desk, Jason."

I smile awkwardly as I stand there like an idiot. "Right, and where was that exactly?"

She turns around, hands on her hips, and points to a desk in the center of the classroom.

"Thank you."

A couple of students laugh at me.

Little shits, you have no idea what I've been through today. I could end you, easily.

The teacher says, "Enough, students. Please quiet down."

The chatter simmers down.

"Now, let's begin. Pass up your homework and get ready for the pop quiz. I want to make sure that you're ready for the big test on Friday."

The class groans.

"Now, now. If you study, this will be easy."

Come on, this is sixth grade math. How bad could it be? I look at the paper being passed out. My mind goes blank the second I see fractions. I don't remember any of this stuff.

"You may begin."

Ok, calm down. I can figure this out. Two-thirds times one and four-fifths. I don't have to change anything to multiply. I just multiply across. Two times four is eight and three times five is fifteen. That's it. I can't reduce it. That wasn't bad at all.

CHAPTER 25

I CAN'T BELIEVE I DREADED THIS stuff as a kid. Try fighting for your life on less than four hours of sleep while simultaneously counting your bullets because you don't have enough. I might actually get good grades this time around.

The teacher begins the lecture on fractions, showing the class what they got wrong on the quiz. I pretend to listen, but a lot of this feels kind of pointless. I've already heard this lecture. I'll use this time to figure out my day. I haven't been here in about six years. According to my planner, my schedule is Math, Social Studies, History. I think lunch was in the middle of the day, followed by PE, English, and finally, Science. I could ask my science teacher about time travel, but I'll have to survive an entire school day to get there. I could try to sneak into a computer lab and use the internet. Google should be around by now. But those rooms were always locked, and I had no means to log into the system. We didn't get student accounts until seventh grade. Fucking bullshit. I won't get a chance to go to the library to check out any books. Five minutes in between class won't be enough time to find anything useful. It was also closed during lunch to keep students from eating there. I could steal one of the rich kid's smart phones. No, that would draw too much attention to me. Plus, I don't think smart phones are that common yet, especially among middle schoolers. If memory serves me right, the first iPhone comes out this year. Definitely too new for middle school kids to have one.

Then again, what do I want? I've traveled back in time. This is a fresh start to a new life. I could just enjoy this, have fun being a kid again. However, if this is the same as last time, then I'll end up in the same place again. I could end up in a horrible repeating cycle. I'll have to do something to change the current path. I need more information first. I'll ask my science teacher at the end of the day about time travel and go from there.

Class ends with us getting a new homework assignment. The day feels like one big déjà vu. I remember so much of this place that I don't even need the room numbers. I know the way, like it's second nature. Next class is Social Studies, technically my elective. Sometimes if the teacher feels like it, we'll have a writing assignment, but this is my goof off class. Rick and I used to just joke around in the back.

Holy shit! I have a class with Rick! I can't wait to see him again… But I watched him die. Should I tell him, or should I just pretend like nothing has happened? I don't think I can pretend. There's just so much that hasn't even happened yet. I'll just come off crazy. I have to pretend.

There he is in the last row, right next to my seat. He seems so happy to see me. The big dumb grin, his blond Afro, and always a collared shirt. He will change to heavy metal shirts in high school. What should I say?

He says, "Hey, man, we missed you in the courtyard today. Where did you go?"

I hide my pinky in my pocket. "Bathroom."

Still smiling, he shrugs and says, "Alright. Did you watch *Family Guy* last night?"

This feels weird. "I've seen every *Family Guy*." Even some that haven't aired yet.

The teacher does attendance and gives an enthusiastic lecture. "Now, I want all of you to write a brief paragraph about how you will shape our world for your future."

That's right, this teacher was obsessed with us thinking about our future. That's why Rick and I always joked around in this class, because it was pointless. Write something generic and you passed.

What were my future plans before the war? I don't think I ever really had a plan.

Everyone takes out a blank paper.

"Now, where will the future take you?"

Rick starts writing, then says to me, "I want to travel the world before I go to college, then become a scientist. What about you?"

What did I say last time? "I don't know."

Did I actually get to grow up? Do any of us? We all get pulled into a war none of us started. All of us die in a fucking meat grinder. Rick does travel the world, until he dies in Egypt choking on his own blood.

I don't want to do this. I know we have to share this paragraph with the class.

The kids on the other side of the room start sharing. Rick is last.

I don't want to do this! I have nothing good to share other than a horrible truth.

Students say their hopes and dreams, and the teacher seems so happy to hear each one.

One kid says they want to go to Harvard and become a doctor that will cure diseases. I see the bloody field surgeons trying to put people back together in Baghdad and can hear the screams. There never was enough pain meds on the front lines. Another kid says they want to be a movie star. I just see another bloody soldier. The draft is going to take you in the first batch.

Then one kid stands straight up with his chest out and says, "I'm Austin Kane, and I'm going to be a soldier like my father before me, because to be born a Kane is to be born a killer."

Wow, everyone in that family really are psychos, even at this age.

The teacher is less thrilled about his answer, but she moves on.

I don't want to do this, please don't make me do this. I look at Rick's paper and read to myself, "I want to travel the world. See Europe, the great pyramids in Egypt, learn Chinese, and see the advanced technology in Tokyo. I want to learn about the world through my own experiences before I learn about them second hand in college." He is so optimistic, though he will one day follow me to his death.

I killed you. I only see his bloody face with popped eyes. "Jason, your turn."

I stare at my blank paper and my eyes feel watery. "I don't want to do this assignment."

She looks disappointed. "Now, Jason, don't be as sour

puss." She makes a large frown to tease me. "Everyone else has shared. It's your turn."

I crumple the paper in my hand, and my voice becomes stern. "No!"

"If that's how you want to be, then you can stay after class and we can discuss why you don't want to participate."

I slam my hand on the desk. "We don't have a fucking future!" I feel everyone's eyes on me.

They look horrified. One girl looks about to cry.

I don't belong here. I stand up and walk out.

The teacher chases after me. "Jason Baker! Where do you think you're going!"

I keep walking. "The nurses office. I don't feel well."

She steps in front of me. "While you're there, you can go to the principal's office."

The principal's office is the greatest punishment for a misbehaving kid, but it holds no power over me anymore.

I stand up straight, half her size. "You want to know about the future? Fine! I have seen it. Hell, I lived it! North Korea nukes Hawaii, and your generation sends my generation into a fucking meat grinder! When you go back into that classroom, remember none of them will live to see the age of twenty." I start to walk past her, then a memory flashes in my head.

This didn't happen last time. I see the nurse's office, then the principal talking to me. I see my next class. I see a fight. New memories flood my mind one after another after another after another, then the light of the bomb flashes in front of me. My head hurts. Two-lifetimes worth of memories are fighting for control in my head.

You don't belong here.

I feel my balance start to go but catch myself. I refuse to fall here. I feel liquid coming from my nose. The teacher is just staring at me. I wipe my nose to see fresh blood. "Excuse me."

She moves out of the way. "Yeah…go."

That wasn't the best move. I should have lied. God only knows what rumors will spread through the school.

The nurse gives me a couple of tissues for my nose. "Don't worry, sweetie. It is the dry season. This happens all the time."

I think it's a symptom of time travel, but there's nothing she can do about it. I probably need a brain scan.

"Your eyes look a little bloodshot. Have you been getting enough sleep?"

"No, not really." You never get enough sleep during a war.

The principal comes in. "I heard someone had a bit of an outburst in class?"

I never dealt with him last time. Principal Sheppard is an unimpressive middle-aged man, balding and unhealthily. Nothing like Drill Sergeant Burns. The very word "principal" is supposed to frighten children. He can't hurt me, just talk and maybe yell. I've been yelled at by truly scary people. Principal Sheppard is no Drill Sergeant Burns.

"Jason Baker, your teacher expressed concern for what you said in class. That you don't believe you have a future."

I say, "Well, sir, we don't."

"You always have a future. You just have to be willing to work for it."

Work for it? I fought tooth and nail for it. What have

you done? I bet you were one of the supporters of the rein-stitution of the draft.

"You're a good kid. Now I'm just going to give you a warning. So stay here, rest up, and then go to your next class." He walks out.

I bet he couldn't handle real violence. Probably would be the first to cut and run.

I go to the restroom to clean off the dried blood and see my face for the first time. I see the child I have become. My face before the scars, before the pimples. So young, but my bloodshot eyes look beyond me. I'm a 19-year-old man who has witnessed the worst of humanity. I've killed so many people, three with my bare hands. I don't belong here, but I don't think I can go back. What the hell am I going to do? I should go home, but I need to talk to my science teacher first. He might have answers, or at least ideas.

CHAPTER 26

THE BELL RINGS AND I have to go all the way back to class to get my stuff. Being this short, it takes a while to get anywhere. I can't wait until I start growing again.

As I grab my stuff from the teacher's desk, she says, "I hope everything is alright, Jason."

I don't stop moving. "As all right as they can be, all things considered." I leave before she has a chance to say more. Tomorrow will likely be very awkward.

I walk in late to my history class, and everyone stares at me. "I'm glad you could join us, Jason. Please take your seat." She gestures to the open seat in the front, saving me the awkward question.

I hear whispers. "Did you hear about his freak out in Mrs. Sinousky's class?"

The rumors have begun. So much for a new start. Now I'm the weird kid. Whatever. Dumb rumors mean nothing. They will be replaced in no time.

History was easily my favorite class in middle school. The history of the world is fascinating. It's an odd thought that I will be living through a historical event in a few years while currently living through my own history, even if it's now slightly different.

Considering history, I think my actions have changed my history. I have a flood of memories from the change, yet I end up in the same place. I still see the light of the bomb. I could use my knowledge to change the future, but how? I have no control over government decisions to go to war. There's also the issue of the bloody nose and the migraine. If I make too many changes, I could completely mess up my brain and end up in a coma.

I'll make a change right now to test this theory, just by thinking about a different outcome. If I think, at least imagine that Rick had a working gas mask in Cairo, he would have lived. I could steal one from our lieutenant. His definitely worked and he only died because his car crashed. Plus, he constantly left his stuff unsupervised. If necessary, I could convince Angel or Luis to help with the heist.

I close my eyes and wait. Where are those new memories? No changes. I still see Rick choking on his own blood from the toxic gas.

Maybe the change only happens through actions and not mere thought. If my actions are great enough, then maybe I can change everything. I could keep Rick from ever joining the army, but I will have to avoid the draft to do that. Telling him now would only freak him out, and I probably already freaked him out with my outburst earlier.

I can see the conversation. *"Hey, Rick, guess what? In 2012, World War III starts and you die within a year, choking on your own blood, so let's get you a working gas mask."* They'd throw me in an insane asylum.

Although that would put me on a new timeline. I could

be happily playing crazy for the rest of my life. No, I could be stuck there for the rest of my natural born life or declared sane and drafted anyway. Plus, Alex and Zack would still die in the navy.

This time travel stuff is too much. I need more info. I need to talk to my science teacher. He's the best option I have right now. I could wait until I got home to use the internet. No, it's 2007. My house won't have decent internet until 2011. My family was a bit behind the times when it came to technology.

CHAPTER 27

Lunchtime! My friends are already at our table eating lunch and talking about the latest episode of some dumb show that will soon be cancelled. They stop and look at me. Rick must have told them what happened in class.

Zack asks, "You doing alright, buddy?"

I take my seat. I want to tell them everything, but I know I shouldn't. "Yeah, for the most part."

Zack says, "I heard you freaked out in class and Mrs. Sinousky gave you a bloody nose."

Great, the rumors have gotten worse. "It's the dry season. Shit happens."

Rick pipes up, "So Mrs. Sinousky did not hit you?"

So that's the teacher's name. "No, just a dry nasal cavity and an unfiltered world view."

Alex says, "You seem different. Your eyes look bloodshot too."

He always was a smart one. Both he and Zack died a world away from me. Stay calm. I might be able to change something, but I have to be smart about it. "Listen, I'm going through a lot right now and I'll let you know when it concerns you guys."

"Alright, sorry for caring." I forgot how snarky Zack was.

I say, "I appreciate it, but there's too much to comprehend right now. Hell, I don't fully understand what's going on. When I have a full understanding, I'll share it with you guys, I promise." I pour out my lunch bag. "Let's change the subject. Has anyone had English yet?"

Alex says we will be reading a chapter from *The Pearl*. The conversation changes as other people join us. I know they all have more questions for me and I want to tell them, but I can't. Not yet.

It has been so long since I had a real lunch, something other than rations and MREs. I swear if I have to eat any more packet peanut butter, I will kill someone. The lunch Mom packed me would look generic to the casual viewer, but to me it is truly beautiful. A turkey sandwich with crunchy lettuce. I haven't had real lettuce in so long. All the flavors complement each other beautifully. A red apple. I had forgotten the taste of fresh fruit. Generic fruit gummies reminds me of the MREs on the front. Zack is disappointed he got a carrot. I hold up the gummies "Want to trade?"

Zack's face lights up with a smile. "Hell yeah!"

You know what would taste great right now? A cold soda. I get in line for the vending machine. I think I'll have a... Oh god, I don't know what to get. I didn't have to make these kinds of decisions for so long. I just ate what I was given. A soda would be good, but what kind of soda? Should I get a Coke, a Pepsi, a Dr. Pepper, or a Mountain Dew? I feel frozen. I can't make a simple decision.

"You going to get something or not, shit head?"

I know that voice. I turn around slowly. Towering above me is the boy who looks like an adult man, Dylan. For a second, fear rushes over me. "No." I quickly make my exit.

To my back he says, "Better move, you little shit."

My fear leaves me. Why am I afraid of him? He's nothing. Just a jerk who's a little bit taller than me. I mouth off, "Fuck off, fagot. You've got plenty of time to wash the taste of semen from your mouth before lunch ends." I know he's homophobic, so that should hit hard.

Dylan yells, "The fuck did you just say to me, you little shit!"

You're nothing to me now, just an angry child with too much strength. I don't hide my smirk when I look back. His fist is clenched, and all his goons look shocked. The sight of all those jerks unable to comprehend that I stood up to their leader is priceless. Then reality hits me like a dump truck. That was stupid. That was *really* stupid. I can't afford a fight right now. Just walk away as fast and as calmly as possible. The second I leave the cafeteria and I know I'm out of view, I book it.

I'm not afraid of him. I'm afraid of the consequences of a fight with him. If we fight, I'll be suspended before I can talk to my science teacher. I also don't know what would happen if I sustained head trauma with my recent memory flashes. It could also trigger a new memory flash. I think I had a flash of a fight, but it's too convoluted with my original memories.

If I stay in the open, Dylan will try to start something to prove how much of a man he is. If I hide somewhere, then I just picked a private place to fight. I need somewhere public and hidden at the same time. I know! I can hang out with the weird kids who listen to heavy metal on the bleachers. It's a decent crowd to hide in and just enough out of view from my pursuers.

There are five of them sitting around a small CD player, listening to Motörhead's *Hellraiser*. I sit down and say, "Sup, I dig the song. Mind if I join?"

They look shocked to have another person want to join them. The one with elbow length black hair and a Slayer shirt says, "It's a free country."

True, until they send us to die. Then the price is our lives.

Dylan and his goons rush out, obviously hunting for me. They search the surrounding fields. I maintain my position with one of the metal kids between me and Dylan at all times. Not too hard, since several of them are rather wide. As it turns out, all of them play in a band together.

"How long have you guys been playing together?"

The Slayer shirt says, "Since summer." He points to his friend in a Slipknot shirt. "Me and Dolton have been playing guitar together for a couple of years, but the band didn't really form until we met Julia and Jake last year." He points to a boy and a girl that look very similar.

Julia says, "My brother plays drums. He persuaded me to join. I sing and play piano. And now we are…"

All of them say in unison, "Green Liar."

The silent fifth member with short red hair pulls out a CD. "We recorded this on my dad's computer." She switches out the disc in the player and turns it on. The recording is messy and low quality.

I see Dylan and lean in closer to the player. Then I hear Julia's voice. She's really good. In that moment, I feel something, something I forgot I had. A feeling that only music can make you feel. I feel happy. Then the bell rings.

I say, "That sounds good. I'll have to catch a live show sometime."

The Slayer shirt says, "We plan to rock the talent show this year."

I don't think I went to that last time.

Julia perks up. "I'll see you in PE."

"Cool, see you there." I had no idea someone in my class was so talented.

I wonder what happened to her, trying to remember what she was like in PE. Then the memories of PE return. The class where my friends and I actively competed against the football kids because no one else did. I have a class with the football kids that are currently hunting for me…

Shit.

CHAPTER 28

I HAVE EXTRA TIME IN BETWEEN classes after lunch and use this time to rush to my science teacher's class. He's standing outside, welcoming his students to his class-room. "Mr. Mayer, what do you know about time travel?" I can't hide the desperation in my voice.

He looks down at me puzzled.

Shit, Mr. Mayer was my eighth grade science teacher. My sixth grade science teacher was Ms. Montoya. She gave us busy work and spent her time on the computer. No wonder I forgot her.

With a cheerful smile, Mr. Mayer says, "I don't know much about time travel, but it might be helpful to look at how films use it. The original *Terminator* films give a great example of a perfect loop. Skynet sends a Terminator back in time to prevent the birth of the leader of the resistance, but instead, the time machine ensures his birth. Then in the second film, they use the remains of the original Terminator to build Skynet, but they cancel that future by destroying all the machines. I also recommend the *Back to the Future* series. They use the knowledge of the future to change everything and make a healthier timeline for the protagonist, plus it has a cool idea for what the future will have. I have to also recommend the *Doctor Who* series. The smallest change in the past can have catastrophic effects on the future. Now, you should get to class before you're late."

I say, "Thank you," and then run to PE as fast as I can.

Mr. Mayer just recommended that I watch several R rated movies to better understand time travel. I can respect that. I've seen most of those movies, having spent too much time in front of the TV as a kid. Maybe I can actually use that to my advantage now.

A small change can have a catastrophic outcome on the future, so I can't just simply save Rick from dying in Egypt. There's no guarantee he would then survive Baghdad. I saw so many die in that city. I have knowledge of the next world war, so maybe it's my job to stop it all together.

I arrive at class just as everyone is let into the locker room. It's always kept locked during lunch to keep students out. Coach does attendance as we enter. I see Dylan's glare and stare right back at him. You ain't shit. He won't try anything in front of the teacher, but I would. Bring it on, you little bitch.

Crap, I have no idea which locker is mine or the combination to it. "Coach…" I think his name started with a W, but I know we called him Coach more than his name, so I'll just stick with that. "Which is my locker and what's the combo? I forgot." I'm not even going to hide it.

He sighs. "I'll check my files."

I follow him back to his office.

"How could you have forgotten it within one day? It's your responsibility to remember these things."

With Coach in the locker room, Dylan won't dare start anything now. This is strategy, you imbecile. I'm not going to fight when my pants are literally down.

Looking through his files, Coach says, "Jason Baker, locker 076, combo 34-5-30."

Christ, I had a lot to remember when I was a kid. "Thanks." I should write that down.

My locker is right next to Rick, Alex, and Zack's locker. I should have remembered that.

Rick asks, "What the hell is going on with you? Dylan was on the warpath, looking for you at lunch. You're like a completely different person from Monday."

I say, "Sometimes people change and not always for the better."

Rick says, "That's fucking dark. What the hell changed in one day?!"

War changed me. Watching you die in front of me changed me. I had to kill every day to survive. I watched cities get bombed into rubble by the machines of war. I saw the worst of humanity tear each other apart limb from limb, all the while praying that it all would end and I could go home. But I can't say that no matter how much I want to. I know they wouldn't understand. So I say, "It was a lot longer than that."

Zack shakes his head. "I recommend you pretend to get sick and bail before Dylan kills you."

I laugh. "Ha! He ain't got the stones to kill. He's nothing but an angry child trying to prove he's a man. He's nothing worth fearing."

Everyone stops talking to me after that. I don't blame them, I'm not the kid they knew yesterday.

Changing into my PE clothes, this body doesn't feel like it belongs to me. I don't have any scars from my prior life, no war wounds. I don't even have my knee scars from mountain biking in high school or my gut scar from running into that barbed wire fence in eighth grade. That was the night Rick and I truly became best friends.

I don't even have my rib scar from soccer. That game is going to happen this month. It will be the last game of the season and because all the other teams have finished, we end up going against an older team and they literally kick the crap out of us. Rick will get a bloody nose, Zack breaks a finger, and I get kicked in the ribs with cleats. This time, however, I'm ready. This time, they won't hurt my friends or me.

We hurry out to the soccer field.

Coach blows the whistle. "You know the drill." He leads us in ten minutes of stretching, then blows his whistle again. "Two laps. Go!"

That's right. PE class always started with two laps around the soccer field. The class takes off running. The jocks sprint ahead. They want to show off to the girls. Some of the other students sprint too but tire quickly. No one ever ran the whole thing. Usually by the second lap, everyone walked. What do you expect? We all have skinny legs. My friends and I would try to mostly stick together, but it took three of my strides to equal one of Alex's.

This time, that whistle triggers something in my brain. I hear Drill Sergeant Burns chant "Mama Mama" and immediately fall into pace with the cadence running through my mind.

> Mama mama, can't you see,
> what the army's done to me.
>
> They put me in a barber's chair,
> spun me around I had no hair.
>
> Mama mama can't you see,
> what the army's done to me.
>
> They took away my favorite jeans,
> now I'm wearing army greens.
>
> Mama mama can't you see,
> what the army's done to me.
>
> I use to date beauty queens,
> now I love my M16.
>
> Mama mama can't you see,
> what the army's done to me.
>
> I use to drive a Cadillac,
> now I carry one on my back.

It repeats in my head for both laps. The jocks say mean shit as I pass, but all I hear is "mama mama can't you see."

Coach gives me a round of applause as I finish first. "Well done, Jason! Where did that come from?"

I was trained to keep going no matter how tired I am,

but I am out of shape. I rush to the drinking fountain instead of answering Coach and suck that water down like my life depends on it. Why didn't I ever bring a water bottle to school? Probably because I was stubborn and/or stupid. I have enough time to catch my breath before everyone else finishes.

This week we're playing basketball. There's enough students for three and a half games. The jocks form their usual team and plan to dominate the game while my friends and I gather the other kids willing to stand against them. The half-court game is all the kids who don't really want to do anything, casually spending the time doing free throws.

Coach will spend the entire class on the bench with the sick or injured students. According to legend, he was a professional athlete back in the day but suffered an injury that landed him as a junior high PE teacher.

By the luck of the draw, we have to play Dylan's jocks on the farthest court from Coach. Alex and Dylan stand in the center, ready for the free through. They're actually the same height right now, but Alex will be taller in the end. The ball goes up and Dylan smacks it to one of his teammates. He tries to make his way across the court, but I snatch the ball from him and take it to the three points line. No unnecessary thoughts, and shoot.

The ball goes in.

Alex exclaims, "Nice shot!"

I played basketball almost every day in Cairo.

One of the goons gets the ball, but Dylan takes it from him. He's so mad, but I don't care. Cry me a fucking river, loser. He rushes for the three point line.

As he shoots, I let out a loud cough and say, "Miss!"

It bounces off the rim, and he curses. Rick catches it. Dylan charges, but Rick passes it to Alex at half-court. He shoots…and it goes in.

"Booyah!" I shouldn't antagonize them, but I'm having too much fun.

Dylan refuses to share the ball until he makes a shot. Here he comes again, and I go for the steal, then WAM. He elbows me in the face, and I fall on my back.

Fucking dick! He takes the shot as my rage seeps out. "Hey, asshole!"

He turns smiling with his perfect teeth.

"You worthless mother fucker!" I punch him in that stupid smile with all my weight behind it. I can feel my knuckles get cut on his teeth. He's dazed and off balance, so I grab his stupid face and slam it into the basketball post. The metal sounds like a gong, and I slam his head again. Die, you worthless asshole. One of his goons tackles me. It's all they are capable of, after all.

My training kicks in. "You're no Hercules!" I roll with the tackle and end up on top. I don't let him think. I start punching. WAM, his nose cracks. "Die!" WAM, cheekbone indents. He tries to block. WAM, I punch through his defense and he's out cold. I reach back to punch again. "Fucking die!"

Someone's arm grabs around my neck and I get yanked back, but the choke hold isn't done right. The arms aren't locked. I easily slide my chin under and bite down hard. The scream that follows is so high pitched, my ear starts to ring. I taste blood and the grip loosens. I put my shoulder in his chest, still holding the arm, and move my hip in to toss my opponent over me. He smacks the ground hard, but I'm not done. I stomp down on his face with all the violence I know.

Whistle sounds grow as two more kids come at me. I hear voices yelling around me.

Two more enemies. I have to finish this before reinforcements arrive. I go for the tallest of the two and take a hit to the forehead to get in close. He shakes his hand in pain. I don't even stagger. A forehead is a thicker bone than a knuckle. I kick this tall bastard's knee in, the crack loud enough for all to hear. He falls screaming bloody murder. The other one looks scared.

I'm not done. I yell with all of my hatred, "Come on!"

He swings with nothing behind his punch.

I catch it, spin around, and simultaneously pull his elbow down on my shoulders while pushing up with my legs. His elbow pops, the crack not quite as loud as the other's knee. I follow with an elbow to the mouth. He starts to fall, but I'm not done. I follow with a haymaker to drive him to the ground while unleashing a battle cry. "Aaahhhhhh!"

The whistle is even louder as large arms wrap around me.

I struggle against the restraint, but I'm not strong enough.

"That's enough!" a booming voice echoes across all the courts.

The adrenaline starts wearing off and fatigue sets in. There are more whistles as several monitors, the school nurse, and both the principal and vice principal come rushing out. Other students cheer, but my friends aren't cheering.

Horrified, Rick says, "Who are you?"

I look back at the carnage I just created. The bodies of

five broken children lie before me. I was so full of rage that I forgot they were children.

Oh god, what have I done?

Coach escorts me to the office with the principal. I stay quiet, nothing to say right now. They couldn't understand my justifications. They sit me down outside the principal's office and go in. I can't hear the conversation.

My hands are shaking and covered in blood. There's a stinging pain on my knuckle and something white sticking out. My fingers move fine, so nothing is broken. I grab and gently pull. Out pops a tooth. I flick it into the nearby trash can. My head hurts, and I feel my mind cloud up. The memories become foggy again. I made another change to the future. I'm going to prison. I end up in the war. Until the light of the nuke brings me back. I wipe the blood from my nose on my gray uniform.

The vice principal speed walks by without stopping to look at me. He goes into the principal's office without knocking and doesn't close the door all the way. I move closer to the door.

"What's the damage report, Greg?"

Vice Principal Greg says, "Well, we've called for an ambulance. By the looks of it, there are five injured. Two broken bones, three with concussions, and several missing teeth."

The principal says, "Jesus Christ, Bernie! Why the hell didn't you stop it sooner?"

So that's Coach's name. "I have plastic knees! I can't move very fast anymore. I also had to fight through a crowd of kids cheering it on. Dylan Bryan and his friends always start trouble in my class. Most of the kids don't like them.

I've sent each of them to you on different occasions. I think it was only a matter of time before they went too far. I missed what started this though. Just saw Jason there smash Dylan into the basketball post as all hell broke loose."

The principal says, "Even if Dylan and his friends are troublemakers, that does not excuse Jason's actions. I'm going to have to call all of their parents and explain what happened, and I trust when the ambulance arrives that the police will arrive with them. This is about to get very messy. We need to get the story straight. Greg, please bring Jason in here."

They're going to call my parents. A few hours ago, I was an innocent child. Now I'm the man the war made. I fought so hard to get home to them, but now that I'm here, I don't belong. God, I don't know what to say.

The vice principal guides me into the office. They sit me down in a plastic chair.

All eyes on me, the principle starts, "So, Jason, I trust you know why you're here."

No, I don't, you fucking idiot. "Because I beat the shit out of five other students."

Vice Principal Greg gasps in shock. "There is no need for that kind of language, young man!"

The principal continues, "Yes, well, you are in a lot of trouble. I'll be calling your parents and the police will also be having a word with you. Now, would you like to explain to us what happened?"

Honestly, no I wouldn't. None of you would under-stand. None of you have ever been in combat. You're just a bunch of figureheads thinking you have authority until real violence happens.

I say, "Dylan elbowed me in the face, and I was tired of his bullshit, so I hit him back and his goons attacked me."

The vice principle says, "Just because someone started it, doesn't mean you have to fight."

Are you fucking kidding me? "And do what? Walk away? That asshole has been picking on me from the moment I met him. Walking away only leaves your back exposed. He started it, and I finished it! Don't talk to me about shit you've only read about. You have no idea how real violence works!"

They look shocked.

Shit, I said too much again.

The principal is the first to break the silence. "Jason, is there an underlying issue? You were always a good kid. What is causing this behavior?"

I cross my arms and look him dead in the eye. "You won't understand."

"This is a safe space. You can tell us if there is abuse in your life."

For Christ's sake. "Dylan has been abusing dozens of students, including me, and you never did shit about it! Well, *I* did something about it!"

They stop trying to talk and send me back outside so they can make their phone calls.

The only person watching me is a secretary on the phone. I could bolt, and they would never find me. I'm trained to live off the land. I could hop the border and escape all of this, including the war.

Then the ambulance arrives with two cop cars.

CHAPTER 29

DYLAN'S MOTHER BURSTS INTO THE office demanding, "How dare that little monster be allowed to stay free! He should be dragged away in chains!" Her hair is messy and her eyeliner is running. She clearly rushed here without a second thought.

The cops try to calm her down. As her husband arrives, he speaks of suing the school and my family into bankruptcy. "How could you let such a violent student into this school!" He slams his fist on the desk. "You will be hearing from our lawyers!"

The principal tries to keep his composure, but I can see he's sweating. "Mr. and Mrs. Bryan, please calm down. We are doing everything we can to straighten this out."

Mrs. Bryan yells, "Apparently not! You have the violent culprit just sitting there. He's nothing but a monster!" She turns her focus to the pair of cops standing between us. "He should be in handcuffs and on his way to prison."

One of the cops says, "Ma'am, it doesn't work that way."

"Well, it should! He harmed my innocent son who never harmed anyone."

She's in a fucking fantasy. "Dylan has harmed almost everyone in our class! He's nothing but a bully! Don't pull that bullshit! He started it! I finished it!"

She grinds her teeth. "How dare you—"

I cut her off. "I dare!" Bring it on, you delusional bitch.

"Jason?" I hear the familiar voice of someone who loves me unconditionally.

"Mom…" She doesn't recognize me, does she? I'm not the son she raised. I'm a soldier forged by war. I want to run to her, but the cops keep me in my seat. I'm sorry, Mom.

The senior officer says, "This is not a simple issue. Based on the stories we have heard from the principle and several eyewitnesses, it appears that Jason here did not start the fight."

Mrs. Bryan tries to interrupt, but the officer continues, "However! His actions were aggressive and based on the damage he caused his fellow students, he is looking at several felony charges of aggravated assault. Due to the fact that everyone involved is a minor, this complicates it further. As well as the fact that the principal here believes Jason was not in a stable state of mind during the incident. I believe that we should take Jason to Juvenile Hall to be evaluated by professionals. They will decide if it is best if he stays there or is released into his parents' custody before his trial."

Mrs. Bryan hits the desk and waves to the cop cars. "Take that little monster away!"

Mom tries to intervene. "I don't fully understand what happened. Jason has never been violent. None of this makes sense."

Mr. Bryan says, "You raised a crazy one, that's what you did."

He only said that to hurt my mom. "Fuck you!" I say. "Don't you dare talk to my mother like that."

I feel a hard smack on the back of my head. "I taught you better than to use that kind of language." It didn't hurt, at least not physically, but I started to tear up anyway.

"I'm sorry, Mom." I grab her for a hug. I don't want to let go, but the cops pull me off and escort me outside, into the hard plastic seat of a police car.

The ride is uncomfortable. The Humvee seats were more comfortable than this. I ask, "Why is the seat made out of plastic?"

The officer says, "It's easier to clean. Some people we arrest are...how should I say this?" He takes a moment to think.

I'm not a child. You can be honest.

"They're really, really dirty and make a horrible mess back there." He shivers, clearly remembering something gross. "Solid plastic is easy to clean with a hose. Sorry for the uncomfortable part."

We sit in silence for the rest of the ride.

I don't want to talk anymore. I stare out the window at my hometown. So many places I've never been to. Stores that I know will shut down in the economic crash of 2008. I fought so hard to get here. This is not how I wanted it to be.

Juvenile Hall is a massive three story building at the edge of town. It towers over me. I don't like this place. It creeps me out. I'm escorted through the lobby. The cops fill out paperwork before taking me down several long hallways. This place must be a mile long. They lock me in a cell alone. Nothing to do but think.

I'm not going to get away with what I did. I beat the shit

out of five children. I probably crippled that one kid when I broke his knee. I'll be convicted of aggravated assault in a criminal court. My family will be sued for damages, as well as the school. If I am getting sent to prison, I'll be there until the war starts and then end up on the same path as last time. However, if I'm deemed insane, I'll end up in an asylum and the military won't look to recruit me. Then I'm stuck there until the war is over, only to watch all my friends die from a padded cell.

I need to stop this war from happening, but that requires my freedom. If I can cause a big enough change, I'll see the results in my clouded memory. So how do I cause that large of a change? I could kill the leader of North Korea. That would stop the nukes from flying in the first place. How the hell would I do that? I would have to get to the other side of the planet, sneak into a hostile nation, and then kill a foreign leader with no money. It would be smarter to bide my time. I have a few years. I can use that time to prepare.

I remember Rick talking about a power dispute in North Korea just before the missiles were fired. I start pacing in my cramped cell that feels rather claustrophobic. I have to turn around every four steps. I think the leader died and his children were fighting with the generals over who would have control. No one knows who actually fired the missiles. I could take out the wrong person. I would have to take out all of them. I need more information. My best bet is to wait a minimum of four years until I do anything rash. I'm twelve now and will hit puberty in three years. I can train my body to be ready for what will be required by the time I'm sixteen. But where will I be?

My memories are clouded. I don't know where I'll be

sent. Prison would be nearly impossible to escape even with my military knowledge and training. I'm willing to bet it would be easier to escape an insane asylum for minors.

It's about sunset, and I'm still alone in this cage. A lesser man would get scared, but I won't be intimidated. I never could sleep well in a war zone. The cell has a toilet and sink all in one. The bed is a raised block of concrete with a thin pad and a blanket. I lay down on the pad. It feels familiar, like my cot back in basic.

CHAPTER 30

THE WORLD IS BLEEDING. I struggle to swim, but the blood is too thick. "You don't belong here!" I fight against the strong current. A sharp pain pierces my left ass cheek, pulling me down. The thick liquid fills my lungs. I cough, but it burns my lungs. "You shouldn't be here!" I see Rick's face floating above me. His eyes pop, pouring more blood, drowning me. I wake up coughing, trying to catch my breath and stay awake until the sun comes up.

Two guards take me to a door that reads Dr. Summers. They wait outside as I go in.

A man in his late forties sits behind a desk with reading glasses on his short nose. "Welcome, Mr. Baker. Please have a seat."

I sit on a big brown couch.

"Sorry for the delay, Jason, but I had a rather long phone call with your parents, as well as your principal and had to have your school record faxed over. All those things took a while. Now then, what can you tell me about yesterday's events?"

Must 'ave been a long fucking phone call. I say, "I got

into a fight with the school bully, Dylan, and I won. Then his goons attacked me, and I beat them. What else is there?"

"I see, but why did you use such violence? You put all of them in the hospital."

The truth will give me an easier sentence. "It's how I was trained." I'll be better off if I go to an insane asylum.

He writes that down. "And where were you trained? I see nothing in your file about special training."

This is the best move for escaping. "Because it hasn't happened yet." I feel stupid just for saying it.

He looks intrigued. "Really now?"

Here we go. "I haven't had enough time to fully understand it, but I am from the future. I arrived yesterday morning, shortly before school started."

He's excitedly writing down every word.

"It's not a delusional fantasy to suppress something. I have too many memories from my life. I know of things that will happen. I know that next week my soccer team will go up against a team of older kids and lose badly. One of my friends will break a finger during the game. I know of an economic crash in 2008 and the next president will be Barack Obama, but I can't prove this stuff until it happens." I sound fucking crazy. Might as well double down. "The world as you know it will come to an end in 2012! I'll be drafted in the next world war. I'll spend the next year and a half in a gruesome battle with Russia and China. I'll see chemical weapons dropped on Cairo. I will witness the absolute destruction of Turkey as it's bombed to nothing but rubble and dirt. I'll be on the front lines for months, fighting for control of Baghdad. I will watch all of my friends die, but here I am, talking to someone who won't believe anything that I say."

He finishes writing. "Of course I believe you."

Fucking liar.

"I have been doing this for a long time. I've seen a case or two like yours in my time. You will come to trust me as we get to the root of what you believe are memories."

I don't like how he emphasized memories.

"Now, tell me, do you remember why you were sent back in time?"

I sigh. Might as well go all in. "I wasn't sent on purpose. I was about ten feet from a nuclear bomb. I remember a bright light, then I woke up on the bus to school."

He folds his hands under his chin. "Well, that is very interesting." He's enjoying the story like I've just told a fairy tale.

I can only hope that will be enough to get me into an asylum.

He makes a quick phone call. "Please send in Mr. and Ms. Baker."

This is going to get messy.

My parents come in, wearing full suit and tie outfits. They wore the same outfits for my grandfather's funeral, which hasn't happened yet.

I think I have three years until then. Holy crap. Grandpa is still alive!

Dr. Summers says, "Hello, Mr. and Mrs. Baker. I'm sorry for the delay. There was a lot of information to gather before I could talk to young Jason."

Mom is angry. "Delay?! It took a full day until I could see my son after a simple school fight!"

"Well, I'm sorry to say things are not so simple."

Dad grumbles, "How so?" He is not happy to be here.

"Your son put five of his fellow students in the hospital. That complicates things. And after talking to him, I believe he might be suffering from a delusional fantasy. He may be a danger to others."

It's not fantasy. If it were a *fantasy*, I would have chosen something a bit more fun. Not a violent war that killed all my friends.

"Tell me, has Jason been playing war games more frequently than normal?"

Dad dismissively says, "No more than I did as a kid. It's normal for boys to play war games. Even if they are video games."

"I see. Has he ever had any kind of martial arts training or been in a fight of some kind before?"

Mom's mouth tightens. "No, never. Him and his older brother will occasionally start roughhousing, but Jason has never been violent. This is the first time he's ever been in a real fight."

From their perspective, true. However, from my perspective, I've been in many fights.

"This is an unusual case, but I believe that you can avoid prison. Give your lawyer these documents and they'll be able to straighten things out." He hands my dad some important looking papers. "You'll be able to discuss their contents with your son and your lawyer. Are you using a public defender, or do you have a lawyer?"

Dad says, "We have a lawyer. My brother will be representing us."

I haven't thought about Uncle Steve since he called me

an unpatriotic coward on Christmas. I wonder how he felt after I was drafted and what happened to my cousins? I never did try to contact them after I was drafted.

My parents and I are left in a conference room with a guard. They read the paperwork from Dr. Summers. There's so much I want to say. I should have written to them more during the war, but I was busy surviving. I don't know how to talk to them anymore. I have to say something though. This silence weighs too much.

I let out a soft, "I'm sorry."

Dad says, "I hope you are. What has gotten into you, Jason? You've never acted like this before. And now we're going to be sued. This is coming out of your college fund, young man."

I had a college fund? I let out a slight giggle.

Mom says, "What's so funny? This is a very serious situation you're in."

I can't hide my smile. I don't know why, but finding out I had a college fund is just kind of hilarious. "I'm sorry, but even now, you two have to realize I have no hope of going to a university. Maybe a community college, but that ain't going to happen either."

My mom looks about to smack me, but Dad gently puts his hand over her hand. She glares at him, but he nods his head to the one guard in the room. She relaxes ever so slightly.

Mom sighs. "Jason, what is going on with you?"

I've chosen the truth once and might as well stick to it. "Well, to be honest, I don't fully understand it myself, but I'm not the son you remember. I'm from the future."

Dad lets out a loud sigh., "Oh Christ." He rubs his eyes. "No. No, you're not."

"I'm sorry, Dad, but I am. I'm from seven years in the future."

He doesn't look at me. "No, you're just confused. You can't justify your actions and are hiding behind a fantasy. We need you to drop the act and maybe we can avoid you throwing away your actual future."

There it is again, *future*. I don't *have* a future. I can't hold it back. "My actual future is on the front lines of a bloody war! I have lived through what is to come. Grandpa will die in three years. The next president will be a black guy and North Korea nukes Hawaii in five years. I watched Rick die in Cairo. I have lived through a war to only be thrown back in time by a fucking nuclear bomb to yesterday morning. Don't treat me like a stupid kid!"

My parents look shocked and concerned.

I feel a pulse in my head. My memories start to fog up. "No, not again. Ahhhhh!" The pain in my head increases as my knees buckle. I see the trial. I see Dylan's parents testify angrily as I'm dragged away. The memories blur, then the bright light of the nuke brings me back.

Mom is holding me as Dad yells at the guard for help.

I wipe the blood from my nose. Sounds are distorted as I clean fresh blood from my ears. They're getting worse. My PE uniform is getting kind of gross. I take a deep breath and stand up. "I'm fine."

Mom testifies, "No, you are not," as she helps me sit back in my chair.

"Every time something changes in my timeline, my memories change with it."

Mom looks at Dad.

I can't see Mom's face, but Dad looks scared.

CHAPTER 31

I T IS AGREED THAT I will stay in Juvy under medical observation before my trial. My parents will talk to Uncle Steve about my case. I am apparently not needed for that. I hate being a kid.

I'm sent to the showers to get clean with cold water and powder soap. They finally give me a fresh change of clothes, an orange jumpsuit that hangs loosely off my small body. Then I'm taken into a section of Juvenile Hall that houses kids my age pre-trial. There are ten cells and a bathroom connected to a community hallway. At the entrance is a corrections officer's desk where they have a perfect view of everything. To his right is a half basketball court surrounded by high concrete walls and a chain link fence roof. An over-weight, middle-aged balding man sits reading from a folder, and every few seconds he glances up at the delinquents in the courtyard.

The guard introduces me, "Bill, I have your new delinquent."

That's unfair. I haven't even stood trial yet.

The corrections officer's voice is hoarse. "I'm reading his file now."

Why haven't I ever read this legendary file?

"Well, Mister Baker, welcome to your new home until your trial deems otherwise." It takes him almost a minute of grunting to stand up. He points out to the kids playing basketball outside. "George, keep an eye out there while I show Jason to his new home. The usual suspects are getting a bit too intense about the game."

As he leads me down the hallway, I smell the familiar odor of cheap cigarettes. I feel a craving. Of all the things to follow me back. I want to smoke a cigarette so badly it hurts. Maybe I can steal one of his or get one from an older kid. They show it in the movies all the time. Cigarettes equal money in prison.

We pass by a girl roughly my current age, reading a chapter book on a beat-up couch. "This is April, one of your fellow delinquents. Say hi, you two."

We exchange an awkward hi before moving on.

"We are coed here. At least until you hit puberty, but don't get any ideas." He turns around, dropping to my eye level at a speed he doesn't look like he has. "I see all! I am your father now, and you will obey my every command. You will make your bed every morning for inspection. Your cell will be spotless and clean. If you fight any of your fellow delinquents, I will bring down punishment far greater and swifter than anything your parents ever did at home. You will refer to me as Mr. Donn and nothing else. You will ask my permission before you do anything. You will ask before touching one of our books." He points to a small bookshelf on wheels. "You will ask permission before going outside."

He points to the half court. "You will ask to go to the bathroom." He points to the bathroom right next to his desk. "You will spend your day outside of your cell, only using it to sleep. Am I understood?"

Honestly, you're not as intimidating as you think you are. Drill Sergeant Burns had the same rules, but he had real power behind what he said. Not just simple threats. Not to mention, Drill Sergeant Burns could probably kill you in one punch while you look like you're about to collapse from the mere effort of standing. "I understand, sir."

My cell is a small space with a simple bed on a concrete slab. There is a sink-toilet hybrid in the corner and a drain in the center of the room. The gray walls tower over me. I feel strangely claustrophobic and hope my trial comes soon. Hopefully, I can get transferred to a psychiatric hospital where I can escape.

We arrive at a clipboard. "Your schedule will run as such. At seven a.m., you will wake up and clean your cell. At seven thirty, your cell will open and you will stand outside of your cell at attention for roll call and inspection. Meals are eaten outside, at the two tables out there, and you will not make a mess, and you will remain seated until I allow you to move. The rest of the day will be determined by me. You will return to your cell at seven thirty p.m. and lights out at eight. Am I understood?"

Again, not much different than boot camp. "Yes, sir." At least I'll get to sleep.

He starts walking back to his desk.

So this is my life until trial. I'm back at boot camp. At least this time I have my own room. I have no idea when my trial is. I have an MRI scan coming up, but again, I have no idea when. I should probably go make myself known outside. Luis told me about his first day in the joint, but he had Angel there to help him. I could go start another fight, assert my dominance, but that would likely hurt my case. I'm an adult. I'll take the high road and avoid any fights these children try to start.

I take a look at the book collection. Lots of young adult books, but one catches my eye. It's a thick chapter book and the spine reads, *Timeline* by Michael Crichton. "Mr. Donn! May I read *Timeline*?"

He hasn't made it back to his desk yet. "Yes, you may. Thank you for asking. Sign it out on the clipboard."

There's a clipboard hanging off the shelf. I sign Lieutenant Baker, then grab the book. The cover is of a medieval knight's helmet with the title across the eyes. I sit down on the couch opposite of April.

I start reading faster than I should, skimming sections of character development. I only care about the science. A soft voice asks something, but I ignore it. It's a thick book, so this will take me a while.

The voice asks louder, "What are you in for?" April has put her book down and is staring at me.

I say, "Aggravated assault against five classmates." Sorry, I'm not here to make friends. I go back to reading, not giving her any more attention.

She asks, "Why?"

She's going to keep asking questions. I close the book with one finger keeping my place. "Because they wanted a fight, and I gave them one." Raising one eyebrow, I turn my attention to her. "Why are you here?"

She hides behind her book, avoiding my eyes, and kind of mumbles and chews on her thumb nail.

I get a flash back to the field hospital. The broken soldier in the padded cell. You're a victim. Well, I'm a jackass. What should I say? I ask in a kinder voice, "Run away?"

She stops chewing on her thumb just long enough to mumble, "Yes…"

I need to change the subject. "So, how long have you been here?" Not very smooth.

She says, "I've been here for about a week, but I'm kind of a regular. Runaways get dropped in here until their parents come to get them."

This is the first time I've talked to a girl since the bunker. The nurses in the field hospital only spent the absolute minimum amount of time on you. Just check your charts, give you meds, and they're gone. That feels sadder than it should be. "Anything I should know about for my first day?"

She looks back at Mr. Donn. "Don't cause problems."

Easier said than done. I put the book in my cell, opting to analyze my new environment. I walk back to Mr. Donn at his desk and stand at attention. "Mr. Donn, sir. I was told I would be getting an MRI before my trial. Do you know when that will be?"

He looks at his computer. "No, I haven't gotten the email yet."

At ease, I say, "Thank you, sir. May I go outside?"

"You may. Most delinquents don't show this level of respect immediately."

I say, "I am more mature than the other delinquents." That's one thing my prior life gave me.

Six kids are playing basketball on the half-court while

two other kids sit at a long metal bench. I can't quite see what they're doing, but it looks like they're drawing. Not much out here, just empty space. Plenty of room to do calisthenics. No real tactical point for escape. Just smooth concrete walls too high to reach.

The basketball players look a bit tougher than Dylan and his goons. One is taller than everyone else by over a foot. He looks like he's sixteen. He's probably been arrested more than once. He steamrolls over a kid half his size to make a basket. He could be a problem. I should avoid him.

Then a familiar face blocks the shot from the big kid. Angel? He has a thin bit of peach fuzz on his upper lip. He was so sad when he had to shave it. I tried to save you. I really did, but I wasn't strong enough. Then the big kid shoves Angel, yelling at him for fucking up his shot.

No! You will not hurt my friend! I run full speed at the aggressive teen, unleashing a battle cry, "Aaahhhhhh!"

I hook my arm around his neck, and his words are cut off as we fall to the ground. I keep my arm around his neck and constrict it using my other arm. He swings his arms, trying to grab me. I kick them away and squeeze tighter. He keeps trying to break my grip, but I'm locked in.

"I won't let you hurt my brother-in-arms! Not this time!"

The kids go from cheering, to worried, to scared. I can see his face turning blue. He's not fighting back as much. He's dying.

Shit. I let go of his limp body, and he takes a deep breath, coughing up chunks of food. I look at Angel. "I've got your back."

He looks confused.

A guard rips me away and throws me in my cell. The solid metal door slams shut.

I only see Mr. Donn's face through a small plastic window.

"I warned you, boy!" He covers the window with a loud thud, and I'm left alone in silence.

CHAPTER 32

NO CONTACT FOR THREE DAYS. I get a tray of food with a cup of water twice a day. They take the old tray when they give me a new one. The taste is on par with MREs. I read through the book in my first two days of isolation. Not much else to do. The hardest thing though, is the lack of sound. The door is soundproof, so I can't hear anyone or anything outside. There's only the buzz of the fluorescent light, which keeps getting louder until it becomes machine gunfire.

"Take cover! In coming drones!"

Where's my gun? Where's my platoon? I'm all alone. I'm trapped. I'm going to die here.

Then the slot opens and food comes in.

I attack it like a wild animal.

What are you doing, soldier? You were trained better than this. What is your mission?

What *is* my goddamn mission?

I look at the book, *Timeline*. "To change time. To stop the war. To save everyone."

I take a deep breath. "Focus, I am Jason Baker. I am not an animal. I am a man. I am a soldier."

I clean up in the sink attached to the toilet and look at my reflection in the metal. My eyes are still the same. "I am Lieutenant Jason Baker of Beta Company Second Platoon. I will save everyone."

I sit on the ground and eat my food in a proper manner. I need to build this body into something capable of making that change as well as strengthen my mind.

I see the mangled bodies from the war until the light of the nuke wakes me. My nightmares wake me every few hours, so I begin my calisthenics. Jumping jacks, pushups, crunches, squats, and, of course, stretching. Making my body strong, keeping my mind focused. My body is becoming lean and strong. Closer to who I was before. I do variants of the calisthenics to prevent injury. Changing hand positions to exercise different muscles in my arms. There is a thin frame above the door I can grab. Pullups with different spacing between my hands. I will need to be able to climb when I escape.

In between workouts, I think about time. Based on my current knowledge, I have a working theory. I need something to write it all down, but until then, I can only think. *Timeline* said it is impossible to travel backward in time, but it is possible to travel to a parallel Earth that exists in our past. You can't travel back to yesterday and kill someone who exists today—that is an impossible paradox. However, I can travel to a parallel universe that exists yesterday and kill someone, which will make a new timeline that exists without that person while the original timeline remains unaltered.

By that logic, my original timeline still exists and is

continuing forward after the nuke while I am in a parallel world that exists in 2007. So, I can't stop the war in my original timeline, but I can stop it in this new one. I wonder if anyone else got sent back as well. I was the closest to the explosion. Austin Kane was there too, but his behavior was normal, even for him. I don't think he got sent to this new timeline. Also, that wasn't the first nuke ever fired. Did this happen in Hiroshima when the first atomic bomb dropped? Trapping people in a loop like this?

I'm going down a dangerous rabbit hole. Back to calisthenics. One hundred pushups. Let's go.

Twenty days later, the door finally opens. Mr. Donn holds his nose. "Eww, boy, you stink! What have you been doing in here?"

I don't answer. Two weeks of constantly working out in the same clothes has left a nasty smell.

They send me to the showers. I'm given clean clothes and made to look presentable, then escorted by a guard to the nearby hospital for my medical examination. Basic stuff for a physical, and they are surprised with how strong I am for my age. After all the standard physical tests, they take me to the MRI machine. I have to lay perfectly still in a dark tube that roars to life. My head feels weird, like it's being pulled in multiple directions. It kind of hurts.

You don't belong here. Who are you? You don't belong here! You need to leave!

I want to scream but my jaw feels locked.

You should be dead! Make it stop, please! Make the pain stop. I don't want this pain anymore! Blackness sneaks into the edge of my vision. My brain feels like it's melting. Then there is nothing but darkness. Nothing at all.

I shoot up, smacking my head on the machine. "Ow!"

The machine is off, and I'm finally pulled out, then taken to an examination room with my parents.

Mom hugs me. "Are you alright?"

"I'm fine." I rub the bump on my head.

Dad speaks to the guard. "This was supposed to be done weeks ago. What happened?"

The guard shrugs. "I'm sorry, sir. Paperwork takes time to process."

"Two weeks to process one piece of paper for a medical examination? What are you idiots smoking to take so goddamn long?"

Mom says, "Honey, language!"

I have heard much worse.

The guard says, "Sir, I have no control over the paperwork, but we are very backed up."

Or Mr. Donn wanted to keep me in solitary to teach me a lesson. I bet he slowed down the paperwork on purpose.

The doctor finally comes in and the guard steps out. "So, we have the results from the scan. Looks like a young healthy brain." He clears his throat. "For the most part." He displays the scans on the wall. The pictures are a bit blurry. "As you can see, the hippocampus is inflamed. It's clearly under a lot of stress."

Dad asks, "What's the hippocampus?"

"That is where all the memories are stored. From the scan, we can tell that it is swollen." He puts up another picture of a brain scan. "This is a brain scan of a child roughly the same age. Look at the difference."

My hippocampus is twice the size of the other scan. "I'm not sure what's causing this," the doctor says. "It will take additional tests, but it is likely why Jason believes he's from the future."

That's what it tells you? This tells me that I have too much strain from the extra memories. If that increases in size too much, I could end up brain dead. I can't afford to have too many new timeline changes.

I ask, "Why is the picture so blurry?"

The doctor says, "This is new technology. The pictures come out a bit fuzzy. However, I will admit this one is a bit blurrier than normal. Possibly some kind of interference." The doctor looks at the chart. "Does anyone in the family suffer from Alzheimer's or memory loss?"

Both my parents say no.

"Hmm. Has Jason ever had trouble with his memory?"

Mom says, "He has always struggled with tests in school."

The doctor rubs his chin, pondering. "This is strange. Very strange indeed. His memory is clearly under stress. This will require further testing." He writes down several things on the chart. Most likely tests I'll have to undergo.

I'm not going back in that machine. "For fuck sake! You're not going to be able to figure it out with the technology of today. I'm from the future. I was right next to a nuclear bomb and my mind was sent back in time. It's crazy, but that's what happened. I have memories from a time that hasn't happened yet and they're competing with the new memories of this past."

The doctor's eyebrows go up, and he writes more stuff down on the chart, then hands the paperwork to my parents. "I recommend a good psychologist. They may be able to figure out what's causing his memories to be overactive."

Before I'm sent back to Juvenile Hall, I finally get to talk to Uncle Steve about the trial. He's less than thrilled. "I don't think this is going to work out well."

Thanks Uncle Steve, even in a new timeline you're a disappointment.

"I'm not a juvenile lawyer and the judge overseeing the trial has a record of giving max sentences. We may be able to plead temporary insanity and get Jason sent to a medical facility, but he is not walking away scot-free."

That's fine by me. My mission is to stop the war.

Uncle Steve does brighten up for a moment. "Civilly, I have you covered. The families are trying to sue for damages, but because Jason is a minor and it was on school property, the school district is liable. They know they will get a lot more money from the district than you, so you should be fine in that department. However, Jason will be expelled from the school district. But we'll worry about his schooling after the trial."

Whatever. I bet I could pass a GED test right now.

CHAPTER 33

THE JUDGE SCOWLS FOR THE entire trial, like he hates being there. Rick is there with his parents, sitting far away from my family. Mom, Dad, and Pete wore nice clothes for the trial, while Annie wore all black with black lipstick and heavy eyeliner. I had forgotten about her goth phase. She stopped wearing that stuff in the summer because black clothes don't mix well with desert heat.

The doctor testifies about my brain scans. The principal testifies about all the kids' school records. Coach testifies about what happened. Then Mr. Donn speaks of my fight on the first day of juvy. Everything goes downhill after that. Dylan testifies that I attacked unprompted.

Fucking liar. He started it.

Then each one of his goons testify that they were trying to protect Dylan.

I'm depicted as a monster. My defense tries to make me seem just unwell. I don't think it worked.

What have I done? I don't belong here with normal people. Maybe I am a monster now.

After my trial, I'm sent back to Juvenile Hall to await

sentencing. Mr. Donn locks me in my cell for thirty days, but I refuse to be broken so easily. I return to my training until the doors open again. How am I going to save everyone if I can't save myself?

At my sentencing, the judge proclaims, "Jason Baker, you are an unwell child. I do not know what caused these sudden outbursts of aggression. You clearly need further medical treatment. However, you have proven to be a danger to others. You have left your victims broken and on the verge of death. With the power granted to me by the state of Arizona, I sentence you to a maximum security prison for juvenile delinquents for the next seven years. You will receive regular mental evaluations and therapy with the chance of early parole in 2012."

In the end, I never stood a chance.

The guards take me away.

Mom cries into her hands as Dad holds her.

Mrs. Bryan yells, "That monster should get the death penalty!"

The judge hits his gavel, demanding order, but she keeps yelling at me.

I should have known it would come to this. I just held out hope that the memories would change, and I was wrong.

They drive me far into the desert, and I'm afraid of what is to come. I'm reminded of my trip from the field hospital, back to the front. I wonder what Meatball is doing right now. I never really learned about his life before the war. Then we arrive at my new home. It looks a lot like a high school, but the key difference is the razor wire fencing. I feel nauseous. My stomach has been turning for the entire ride.

Just breathe. I can't let my nerves get to me.

I'm introduced to my new corrections officer. This guy takes way better care of himself than Mr. Donn, but he's no Hercules. "Welcome to your new home, Jason. I am Mr. Brook, and you may only refer to me as Mr. Brook. Now, you are one of the youngest delinquents I have seen, but you are not the youngest and you will not receive special treatment for your age. You will be treated the same as the other delinquents. Treat others with respect, and you will receive it. Act right, and your stay will be a shorter one. Understood?"

The world is depending on me making parole, even if it will be cutting it short.

"Yes, sir." I'm getting really tired of saying that.

I'm given a blanket and prison clothes, then Mr. Brook escorts me to B-block, which is a long hallway with bunk beds on both sides and six tables down the center row. There are no cells. Looks like my barracks in boot camp, except there we were all the same age. Here, I feel very small. These don't look like juvenile delinquents. They look like grown men smoking cigarettes, working out, and talking in packs. All their eyes focus on me, the new fish. I'm escorted to a bunk in the middle of the left side.

"Here you are. Make yourself comfortable." Then he just walks away.

My bunkmate is on the top bunk, reading a book, and looks to be about fourteen. His clothes look a little too small for him. He probably just hit a growth spurt.

"Welcome to B-block. What are you in for?" He doesn't seem to care, only asking out of necessity.

I unpack my things. "Aggravated assault on five…no, six people."

He closes his book and leans over the top bunk. "Really?"

I answer, "Yeah." I make my bed.

"Most people say an accident or that it wasn't their fault. My last bunk mate accidentally ran over his neighbor." He grins. "He hung himself about a week ago."

I look at him. "And what was your accident?"

Still grinning, he says, "I accidentally burned down part of my school. I had no idea playing with matches and kerosine could be so dangerous." His smile says otherwise. "I'm Poco."

"Jason."

He takes out a pack of cigarettes. "You smoke?"

I want to take it so bad, but I say, "No, I have a mission. Can't compromise it."

He pulls back. "Are you a snitch?"

I give him my crazy smile, showing off my crooked teeth. In another time, I got braces in eighth grade. "No. I have to stop the third world war."

He looks concerned.

"Sorry, but you're stuck with a certified crazy."

He keeps an eye on me but goes back to reading his book.

I'm used to no privacy. You lose all sense of that in the army. However, these delinquents aren't fellow soldiers. They look at me as if I'm a small piece of meat. They look tense, almost ready to pounce. I don't want trouble, but I am more than prepared for it.

Poco says, "Here comes Jordan."

"Who?"

Suddenly, I'm surrounded by five large delinquents. They tower over me by multiple feet. The largest, a very beefy black teen, steps a little too close for comfort. "Hey, new fish." The malice in his voice smacks me in the face.

I say, "I'm not looking for trouble." I don't think I put enough fear into that but hope they bought it.

Jordan leans down closer, putting his face within striking range. "Listen, pip-squeak. There is a pecking order around here. We are at the top, and you are at the bottom. So whatever we say, you do."

There are two people in a fight, the quick and the dead. I'm quick. I grab his ears, pulling his head into my forehead. I caught him off balance, because he wasn't expecting a fight yet. I feel a pop and warm liquid spurt onto my head, then kick him in the balls for good measure. His friends swing at me. I use my size and speed to duck under the punch, but I am getting overwhelmed. Another punches me in the face, and I might as well have been hit with a cinderblock. Black spots form on the sides of my vision.

Stay conscious, damn it!

A tight grip wraps around me, pinning my arms down. I feel my breath get squeezed out of me.

Fool, you should have gone for a choke.

One of them gets in front and punches me in the face again. I feel my jaw shift and my teeth loosen.

This was a bad decision.

No, damn it. Keep fighting! Never give up. Find an opening.

I kick the one in front with both feet. He steps back, avoiding me but ready to strike. I grab the pinky finger of my grappler and bend it the wrong direction until I hear a snap. His grip loosens, and I slip out. The others charge, and I can't take them both. I use my height difference to avoid being surrounded again. Then the one with the broken finger hits me in the ribs and I lift into the air, the air in my lungs knocked out of me. I can't breathe. I stumble into one of the tables in the center of the corridor with a loud clang. I can't catch my breath.

Come on, focus.

I force myself to exhale, resetting my breathing. Air re-enters my lungs, and I stand up. All five of them stand in front of me. Jordan stands in front with blood dripping from his nose and rage in his eyes. I spit out my loose teeth and put my arms up, ready for more. It's too late to back down now.

I yell, "Come on!"

Everyone else in the barracks starts chanting, "Fight!" in unison.

Whistles sound off as the corrections officers come in. I've run out of steam. They put me into solitary confinement. The silence slowly sinks in as the adrenaline fades from the fight. I don't like the silence.

CHAPTER 34

RETURN TO MY CALISTHENICS EVEN though my face and body hurt. My left eye and jaw are definitely swollen. I spat out a molar and now wonder if it's the same one I lost in Baghdad. I must train through the pain. Jumping jacks and shadow boxing, my form is lacking. I hear a muffled scream from another person in solitary. I hesitate in my routine as a memory I would rather repress flashes in my eyes. I'm back in Baghdad. Someone is screaming for help, but I can't get to them.

No, I'm here now. Stay focused.

There is another scream. He's hurt, somewhere close, just around the building.

"No, focus on something else." I drop to the floor, covering my ears as I do crunches.

I still hear the screaming.

"Shut up! You're not helping."

Just push through it. Keep training.

The screaming just won't stop.

I can't reach you, there's too much in the way. "I'm sorry!

I can't save you! Please just stop! Please just make it stop!" Make the voices of the dead stop.

There is nothing here but the sound of the dead. They surround me in the dark. Reaching out to me with their dark hands. One stands above me. "You're running out of time."

"I know."

"If you don't stop it, all our deaths will be your fault."

"I know." I'm trying, but I can't do anything from here.

I float alone in a sea of the dead. Millions cry out. There are so many. The tsunami of death crushes me. I gasp for air in the dark room, still in solitary. My nose is dripping with a dark liquid. There was no memory flash that time. I'm running out of time. I get out of bed and begin my calisthenics. I must train.

They are always calling to me, so many voices saying, "You're failing us."

I've lost the night Rick and I became best friends. I will be in prison when Pete was supposed to take us to a high school party. I will no longer run into a barbed wire fence while escaping the cops. Rick won't treat my gut wound. I still remember it, but it will never happen.

The light of the bomb is still in my future, the only true constant. I can't remember what Zack wrote to me. I'm failing. I'm forgetting their sacrifices. I have to save them. I'm the only one who can. I have to tell myself that over and over again. I have to save them. Millions of lives depend upon me. I have to remember., I have to train. I have to get out of this room!

"Let me out! I have to save everyone!"

My head hurts. The pain is always there. Remember, always remember, even if the future fights back.

CHAPTER 35

THIRTY DAYS LATER, THE DOOR finally opens. I'm sent back to B-block. They stare at me with less hungry eyes and whisper to each other. I can guess who's the topic of that conversation.

Poco is reading a new book and casually says, "Did you enjoy the vacation rooms?"

I say, "I need a notebook, a pencil, and a book on physics."

He closes his book. "What for?"

"I'm going to prove I'm from the future."

He says, "Seems quiet time hasn't helped your mental state. Hmmm…those aren't contraband, so they should be easy to get. You can buy school supplies from the store."

My parents won't want to fuel my delusion. "I don't have any money."

He says, "You can get a job here." He points to the front of our complex. "Just ask the guard at the front desk what jobs are available. Better sign up quickly; otherwise, you'll get stuck on toilet cleaning duty." Then he points down the hall. "Check the library for any physics books."

"Thanks. I hope I didn't cause any trouble for you with my fight."

He shrugs and goes back to reading his book. "It don't mean nothing. I'm almost out of here anyway."

I finally get to meet the resident psychologist. She's writing something in a file as I'm brought in. Her hair is light brown with lots of gray strands. She glances at me through thin reading glasses. "Hello, Jason Baker," she says with gum in her mouth.

The guard leaves us alone.

I say, "Hello," not really sure what else to say.

She doesn't look at me, just keeps writing. "How are you doing today, Jason Baker?"

"Not great, but I'm here." Fairly honest.

"And how is the future, Jason Baker?" she says with such a lack of emotion, I squeeze the chair, hoping it will keep me from smacking her.

"It's still bad. Nothing's changed. What the heck are you writing?"

She keeps writing. "You missed the last several sessions, and I have to fill out these forms for your absence. These take time, and I have a lot to fill out. You're not the only one who skips these sessions."

"Are you fucking serious?"

She points to a sign on the wall that says, Profanity Free Zone, with a sad kitten in the center.

"Fuck your stupid fucking sign! I asked you a question. Are you fucking serious? I've been in solitary fucking confinement for the past four fucking weeks!"

She puts down her pencil and, in a calm, condescending voice says, "Jason Baker, there is no need for such language.

You chose to get in a fight, and as a result, you paid the price. You missed your mandatory session because of your actions. Such actions reflect badly upon you. You must learn that your actions have consequences."

I stand up. "Fuck you!" I could kill her right now. She has scissors on her desk. It could all be over in a few seconds. I should show her exactly what I am. Instead, I take a deep breath. "I was trained to fight so people like you could stay home, safe from the horrors of war. Now, I'm in a situation that calls for me to fight or be abused. You don't understand, and you clearly don't want to." I slide the paper away from her and grab the sharpie next to the scissors. I write on the paper in bold letters, FUCK YOU, then walk out, sliding the sharpie into my pocket.

I go by the library before returning to my bunk. There's a whole section of out of print old textbooks where I find an introduction to physics book printed in 1984. Old, but it will have to do. I may be bad at tests, but I am good at doing the work. I have five years to figure it out. I hope I can do it. Otherwise, I'll have to do something absolutely insane.

Back at my bunk, Poco says, "You left early?" He's still reading his book.

I kick the metal frame of the bunk. "Fuck that bitch!" My toe hurts now, which fuels my frustration.

He laughs. "No one likes her. I've yet to meet a single person to sit through a whole session. We think she does it on purpose to work less."

I sigh. "I'm not getting out on parole, am I?"

He shrugs. "Probably not. You did get in a fight with the big dogs on your first day, which is actually a smart move."

I'm shocked. "It was?"

"Hell yeah. You would have been someone's bitch otherwise. You're a little kid, and everyone here wants to prove they're a man, especially Jordan. He has been the top dog here for the past three years. He's never lost a fight. Now, some little kid took him on. You put a crack in his image. He can't attack you because you're just a little kid, but he has to prove he's still on top and that makes everything complicated. But you should still watch out for Marcus."

I quickly scan my surroundings. "Who's Marcus?"

Poco hops off the top bunk and points to the largest teenager I've ever seen. He could easily play a linebacker for college football.

"Sweet Jesus."

Poco adjusts my gaze. "No, wrong guy. That's the giant. He's not the one to worry about. He's in for beating up a mailman." He points me to the teen next to the giant, a lean teen with patchy stubble. "That's Marcus, and he's in for sexually assaulting two boys."

Marcus looks right at me with a devilish smile and winks.

A chill runs down my spine. My head throbs as a new memory flashes. It's dark. Someone has their hand over my mouth. I struggle as several other hands hold me down. Oh God, he's going to rape me. I feel blood seep from my nose.

"Him and two others are in here for sex crimes. They stick together and help each other get their rocks off. They're all fucking creeps. The only reason they haven't tried anything on you yet is because of your fight."

I'm already running at Marcus intent to kill. "I won't let you!"

Unprepared, Marcus scrambles for something in his

pocket. Before he grabs it, I've slammed into him at full speed, grabbing one leg and sweeping the other. He is no Hercules and falls to the ground.

Everyone backs away, not wanting any part of this.

I scramble to get on top, yelling, "I won't let you!" as I start punching.

His face quickly decays into a bloody mess, but then he catches his breath and shoves my small body away. He pulls a sharp piece of metal from his pocket. Blood drips from his mouth as he slashes wildly at me. My training kicks in as he stabs down. I grab the arm, slipping past his guard, and use his own momentum against him, pushing him into the metal bunk bed. With a loud clang, his arm goes limp and he drops his weapon.

He spits out, "You worthless piece of—"

I stomp down hard between his legs.

He lets out a gasp as tears fill his eyes.

I grab his dislocated shoulder, squeezing it to get my point across. "If you ever look at me like that again, I will kill you." Then I smash his head back into the bunk bed. That will send a message to everyone that I am not to be messed with.

Blood drips from my nose. Marcus's nighttime assault becomes a memory of another time. I made a positive change.

The guards come running in, ready to break it up, but it's over. They're always just a little too late.

I say, "The knife was his," as I'm dragged back to solitary. I've yet to actually sleep in my own bunk.

CHAPTER 36

'M BACK IN ISOLATION WITH nothing but my thoughts again. I should not have rushed into that. I was so blinded by my rage that I stopped thinking. I could have been more strategic. I could have learned his patterns and taken him out without anyone ever knowing. Why the hell didn't I wait?

"God damn it!" I punch the metal door with my anger behind me.

I attacked out of revenge as if he had already assaulted me. He was going to do something terrible to me. All I know is violence. It's the only solution I know how to use. I punch the door again and again and again until my hand is a bloody mess.

I pull out the physics book I had stuffed into my waistband as body armor and drop it on the bed, realizing I thought to use body armor even without a real plan of attack. I have nothing else to do but study now. I'm also stuck in prison until I reach nineteen again. Maybe I can…

Two knocks sound at the door. I hide the book under the bed covers before it opens.

In walks a white-haired man in a full suit and bolo tie. "Jason Baker, you are proving to be quite a troublesome inmate. On your first day, you get into a fight with several older teens. Then as soon as you are allowed to rejoin your fellow inmates, you insult our resident therapist and attack another inmate. You're clearly a danger to those around you. In an ideal world, we would lock you away from everyone and you would be forgotten, but new legislation prevents us from leaving anyone in solitary confinement for longer than thirty days. And due to an overflow of delinquents, there is nowhere else to send you. Now, your latest fight is a bit confusing. You attacked a fellow inmate unprompted, but he had a weapon on his person. Now, this weapon could not be yours due to how little time you have been among your peers. Having any kind of weapon is a major violation and receives severe punishment. So, now I ask, why did you attack Marcus Napier?"

You just love to hear yourself talk, don't you? "Well, first off, sir, who are you?"

He smiles. "My apologies. I am Warden Tibias Fox. Now, why did you attack Marcus and put him in the hospital wing with a fractured skull and dislocated shoulder?"

I look him dead in the eye. "Because he was going to rape me tonight. I chose to make a preemptive assault for my own protection."

His face becomes stern. "Really, and how did you know that?"

Don't use the future as an excuse. It's not going to help. "Are you aware of his reputation, sir?"

He nods. "I am."

"I am the youngest and the shortest one here. I'm a

target. If I don't fight with everything I have, then I will be the victim of horrible things."

He nods. "I see." He pauses to think for a few moments. Did that work?

He says, "I understand where you are coming from Jason, truly I do. But you cannot solve all of your problems with violence. The outside world doesn't work that way. You have to learn to talk out your problems. You may have that to think about for the next thirty days. Your family has tried to come visit you, but due to your actions, you have been in solitary every time. They left a letter for you. You can have it after you finish this next stretch in solitary." He turns around and leaves.

The door locks behind him.

The world doesn't work on violence? Violence is all I know. Violence is how I was trained. The world needed young men to be violent to solve its problems. You know nothing of the violence to come. I wasn't going to let that creep have his way with me while everyone pretended not to hear. No, I don't regret what I did. I changed the future with my actions because I chose to attack, and I will do it again.

"I will change everything! I have the power!"

I pull the physics book from under my bed covers and the sharpie from the therapist out of my pocket. I will prove the existence and demonstrate the power of time travel and then will use this knowledge to change everything.

A flash of new memories flood my mind as I study the physics book nonstop. There's so much to learn. So many formulas and theories within one textbook. I study all I can until the light of the nuke brings me back. I stumble out of bed, barely holding my stance. Blood drips from my nose.

My head throbs with pain. I've read this book cover to cover in another life, but it wasn't enough.

Fine! I'll work it out one step at a time.

I draw a diagram on the wall of how far away I was from the bomb. Best guess, I was about ten feet away. I was most likely hit with a thermonuclear bomb, which could have released anywhere from fifty to one hundred kilotons of energy. One kiloton equals a thousand tons of TNT. I can compare that to the bombs I saw dropped in Turkey. Back in boot camp, they taught us what to do in the event of a nuclear detonation. "Evacuate to a minimum of ten miles and seek shelter." So past ten miles is survivable.

There are five thousand, two hundred eighty feet in one mile. Austin Kane was about fifty to one hundred feet from the explosion and that was far enough away to not send him back, or at least not to this timeline. For all I know, he will be brought back within a year or so, but I will never know locked in prison. Not to mention, he won't even think about stopping the war. Judging by that family motto, he will just be looking forward to fighting all over again.

From a tactical point, the explosion was to destroy the city and damage two armies. Without a missile trail, the Chinese have plausible deniability. They could blame a third party, like a terrorist group. The bomb was likely an older model. It would have been a waste to use a brand new bomb in such a location. Save the more powerful bombs for major cities.

God, what is happening in my original timeline?

If safety is ten miles from the explosion, I can divide that into five sections at a distance of two miles each. I diagram the sections in my drawing on the wall. There were American and Russian troops within sections three, four, and five. Section five most likely had several inbound helicopters and outgoing planes. The Electro Magnetic Pulse would have taken out anything electrical in section five and beyond. I was in section one as were any survivors of the initial bombing. The collapsed entrance was about fifty feet from the bomb. I was the closest, so I got hit with the most energy. At ten feet, I went back six years. I don't know the exact time of detonation, so I'll have to stick to rough estimates. I would say it was mid-day, early afternoon. Let's say twelve to keep it an even number. I arrived about thirty minutes before the first bell. Middle school started at seven thirty. I don't remember what day it was before the blast because days blended together in the war. Rough estimate, I traveled back six years, four-ish months, and five hours at ten feet from the blast.

All this thinking is making my head hurt even more. Christ, there's just too much!

I see carnage of Baghdad from a different angle and feel the blades pierce my flesh again. The see faces of the men I killed, their last moments of fear and pain. I'm back in the fight, bleeding and crying for help. Don't leave, Angel! We still need you. I run into the building, meeting the light on purpose.

I'm on cold hard concrete, moon light illuminating the cramped cell. My nose is crusty with dried blood. It's impossible to tell time in solitary. No clocks or calendars, just a tiny window too high to reach. I rub my nose only to find fresh blood just under the surface. The sharpie has dried out. Fucking typical. Blood leaks into my mouth.

Use whatever you can to complete your task.

With my blood as ink, I start writing formulas from what I know now and what I knew from another lifetime. I have to figure out the energy. What's that Einstein equation? $E=Mc^2$, but what does that mean? I thumb through the book, leaving bloody fingerprints all over it. Here we go. Energy equals mass times the speed of light squared. Applying that to my situation, I determine the energy of the explosion, several kilotons, equals my mass at the time, around one hundred sixty pounds of just body weight, times the speed of light squared.

Wait, that can't be right. My whole body didn't travel back in time, just my mind, but not the brain itself, just my memories. And they are changing constantly with each change to the timeline. Then maybe it's the energy of the explosion unleashed at a distance of ten feet equal to the mass of my memories moving at the speed of light backwards squared. It could be both the energy of the nuke and the energy of my consciousness, plus the mass of me, times the speed of light squared.

I'm close to the answer. I just need the right numbers. I keep working out the equations over and over again. I can see it, but it's just out of reach. I can see time. My constant memory shifts illuminate the flow of time, and I live through another life of fighting and studying only to be met with the light of the nuke. Memories from different lives shape me into someone else. I can never save everyone. If Rick doesn't join with me, he dies on a different front. If he does and I get him past Cairo, he dies in Baghdad. Everyone always dies in Baghdad. The fight is always too chaotic to predict anything.

After watching everyone die dozens of times, I change

to a new set of equations and a new set of memories is sent back with the explosion of the nuke, the only true constant. I have to make sure the nuke sends me back or else darkness will fill my mind. But the light never fades away.

The door opens. "Good lord! What have you done?"

I don't look to see who it is. I've been getting new memories nonstop and the days no longer matter.

They yell, "I need help escorting Jason Baker to the medical wing immediately!"

I keep working, desperately trying to finish. "Wait! I'm so close! This is the answer to time travel. The proof is here!"

Guards grab me.

I hardly ate any food and couldn't waste the juice when I was so close to finishing. The blood loss has stolen some of my strength as well. I know I'm in no shape to fight, but I'm so close.

"Wait! Don't destroy it! This will change the future!"

They don't care. They're already calling for cleanup.

Warden Fox looks at me from down the hall. I see him mouth the word, "Disappointing."

The guards are strong, but I use my sweat to slip through their grip. I try to reach Warden Fox. "Please, Warden! This will change everything. This will save everyone!"

Then my head throbs and my memories begin to burn with the heat of the bomb.

I cry out, "Please!" but I have grown so very weak.

My consciousness begins to fade into the many lives I have lived as darkness takes me.

CHAPTER 37

I HAVE BEEN STRAPPED TO A hospital bed and on an IV drop for days, though I don't know how many. The worst thing is the bed. It's too soft. I'm used to sleeping on the ground or the lumpy pad on concrete in solitary. This feels like a cloud that I'm sinking into. It's just too damn soft.

I stare out the window at my clear view of the garden, where delinquents work the desert land to grow plants and crops. Can't imagine the dirt here is very fertile. However, that can't be too bad of a life, growing food for a living. Everyone has to eat. My job wasn't needed, was it? Just another kid turned into a killer. I wish I went home after the war, settled down to an honest job and built my own family. I wish I hadn't been sent back. Now I carry the knowledge of having failed everyone.

"Jason Baker, are you awake?" says the only female voice in the complex. The therapist who's name I forgot because I had more important shit.

Why does everyone here use my full name? It's kind of annoying. I don't look at her. "I'm awake."

She says, "Jason Baker, I was informed by Warden Fox that you made a bit of a mess in solitary confinement."

I turn to her, not hiding the anger in my voice. "That wasn't a mess. That was math! Mathematical proof of time travel!"

She nods her head. "Uh huh." She scribbles something down on her clipboard.

I turn away from her. I hate just looking at her. "What are you writing down? Actually, I don't care. You don't believe me, and you don't want to. This is nothing but a paycheck to you."

"So tell me what caused you to want to deface your cell and ruin a book that doesn't belong to you."

Why don't you care? It's literally your *job* to care. "I'm trying to change the future. Those equations were proof that I'm from the future. Proof to stop the war." My head hurts. My eyes feel wet. "But you don't care, do you? Everyone is going to die, and you don't care." I feel the tears run down my face. "None of you care. Lock the crazy kid away and forget about him. That's the easy answer, isn't it?"

She says, "Jason Bak—"

But I cut her off with a scream. "Shut Up! Just leave! Make up whatever bullshit you want to so you can feel better about yourself! The war is still going to happen, and you're going to send everyone in this place to an early grave! Leave, you fucking useless bitch!"

She gets up.

I keep yelling as she leaves, "Get the fuck out of here!" I'm twisting and turning against my restraints, but they're too strong.

I give up. What's the point anymore?

After several days in this uncomfortable bed, the doctor sends me back to B-block. I get the same stares as last time. No one dares confront me. Not that I'm strong enough to fight this time.

For the first time, I sit down on my bunk. Christ, my head hurts.

"So you're the crazy one I've heard about."

I know that voice. "Angel?"

"How do you know my name? Wait, you're the guy who choked Neil back at juvenile hall."

Joy fills my heart for the first time in so long. My friend from the war.

He jumps down. "Why did you do that?"

I pull him in for a hug. "I'm so happy to see you."

At first, he freezes, not sure what to do. He quickly gains his composure and pushes me off, then stands ready to fight.

I say, "Sorry, I've been in solitary for the last sixty days. It's good to see a familiar face."

He looks confused.

"I know it doesn't make a whole lot of sense right now. Just know that I have your back no matter what."

Still looking confused, he says, "Cool...thanks," and then carefully moves past me to leave.

Angel is the same age as me. Why is he here with all the violent offenders? He was in for selling drugs, and as Luis told me, his father was the one pushing it. "Wait! Angel, why are you in B-block? Your offenses were for drugs?"

Angel stops, turns around, and gets right in my face. "How the fuck do you know that?"

I struggle to think of a logical explanation. "A mutual

friend told me." A mutual friend that neither of us have met yet.

He grabs my shirt collar. "You don't know a goddamn thing." He storms off but is cut off by the same pack of teens that harassed me on my first day. Jordan's nose is still kind of crooked. "Where *you* going, little Angel?"

Angel is surrounded and takes a defensive stance.

I yell, "Hey!"

Everyone turns to look at me. I'm not strong enough for a fight, but I would gladly die for my brother-in-arms. I say with all the strength I have, "Angel's off limits!"

We stare each other down for a solid minute.

Then they back off, Jordan saying, "We don't need this shit right now."

Angel looks back at me still not sure what to think of me.

I see his future, the great leader he's meant to become and the bloody death he will suffer. I have to save him.

CHAPTER 38

GET A JOB CLEANING THE bathrooms. Everyone treats it like the worst job in the world, so it usually has to be assigned to someone. I don't mind. It reminds me of basic training, except without Drill Sergeant Burns yelling at me. I can shut my brain off and just clean. Finally, for that short amount of time, my head doesn't hurt and the weight of the future lifts for just a moment.

While I'm mopping, a group of ten teenage delinquents comes in. My survival instincts kick in instantly. There is only one door in or out and no guards or cameras allowed in except during emergencies. I move quickly and deliberately, putting my back to the wall and my mop bucket between me and the teenagers. I then detach the wet mop head from the wooden stick. I can't beat them all, but I can get through that door before they overwhelm me.

However, they don't charge me. Instead, they circle around two delinquents. Jordan from my first day and a lanky Hispanic teen.

Jordan says, "You crossed the fucking line, wetback!" His crooked nose feels like it's looking at me.

The lanky Hispanic says, "Fuck you, Jordan! I ain't giving you shit. You're not the top dog no more."

Jordan throws the first punch. He's met with a return punch. Soon the fight devolves into a chaotic fury of punches, neither willing to give an inch. Their uncontrollable fight throws them at the surrounding delinquents who simply step aside, refusing to help either one of the combatants.

Not my fight, not my problem. I quickly make my way to the door where a singular delinquent stands guard, peeking out a small crack in the door. He puts his finger to his lips. I nod that the message is clear, and he lets me out. I put away my cleaning supplies while taking several deep breaths to collect myself.

Holy fucking shit! That could have gone a lot worse.

CHAPTER 39

THE ORCHESTRA OF DEATH DEAFENS me as the millions of decaying corpses surround me. "You're failing us!"

I hold my ears, but it's too loud. I know, but I can't do anything. I'm trapped.

Rick reaches out, his eyes red with tears of blood. "Don't let me die!" His voice is hoarse.

I grab his hand, trying to pull him free. but his grip goes limp. Yellow gas seeps out of his body as it is pulled back into the sea of the dead. I look over at Angel fighting off the dead as they pull him down.

I can save him. He's so close.

Knives stab him as he cries for help.

I can save him. I'm so close!

"Don't leave me!" comes Luis's voice, but he's so far away that I can't save them both.

I'm so close to saving Angel, but I can't abandon my friend. I can't save them all!

My eyes open, my gaze falling on my own outstretched

hand in the darkness. The dead always wake me around three in the morning.

I take my notebook from under my mattress. The only light source in B-block is the guard's station next to the main door. In the small yellow light, a guard in his early twenties sits reading a book. He sees me approach and nods his head, then continues reading.

Already sitting on the floor under the guard's light is a thin teenager drawing. He doesn't look at me. I sit down next to him. He's sketching the image of a man having a chainsaw shoved up his rear end. We don't need to talk. We sit in silence until the sun rises, each working out our pain in our own way.

I'm thirteen according to this current timeline, but I have memories from many other lives. That's the sad truth behind time travel. You can't travel to your past. You can only travel to a parallel world existing at a different time. As a result, my memories take over the version of me that originally inhabited this body. Through the memories of my war experiences, he becomes me. Then all the other versions come back, giving me knowledge of my many failures. That's what I was missing with the equations. I am nothing more than the collections of the many short lives of Jason Baker. I chose to enter the room with the nuke in other lives to ensure this version received more knowledge. As I finish the math in my notebook, my mind flashes with another life of war. I'm trapped behind bars until the war starts and can't tell the truth to anyone to make a difference.

When the sun finally rises, I've finished the equations in my notebook. I just had to rewrite them, and that took a longer than I thought. The nice thing about math is it can only be worked out one way, if done correctly.

We line up for inspection before we can eat. After eating, they send us outside. It's a nice day. Not too hot, with a cool breeze. I start my work out. No one bothers anyone during a workout. It's the only courtesy of this place. When I finally stop to catch my breath, my mind falls into deep thought again.

Why can't it be simple? All it takes is for someone to read the notes and the truth is literally spelled out. The world can then focus on new technology and distracting North Korea from firing that nuke at Hawaii. My high school friends won't die in the third world war. Meatball can live a happy life, doing whatever he does. Although, Angel drifts in and out of prison for the rest of his life because his father keeps using him to move drugs and will likely continue down that path because it's all he knows. I would rob him of his glory from finding his true calling as a leader, but he would be alive. Then there's Luis. I can't manually save him from stealing that car while I'm trapped in prison. Then if I stop the war, he will spend his life in prison rather than die in a war far from home.

Angel has a short sentence, but he will be busted again within the next three years. Luis will be arrested in four. I could convince Angel to get away from his father's influence, try to give him a chance at a free life. Then who would be here for Luis? If I stop the war, I will be out of here at eighteen, leaving Luis to fend for himself for the next twenty-five years. I could cause more trouble in order to extend my sentence to protect him.

Stopping the war will mean that I won't get sent back in time. That will darken my mind, either killing me or putting me in a permanent coma. My life is forfeited anyway. I'm nothing but a violent monster now. I can't function in normal society anymore. Darkness is all I can hope for, but I have to save the ones I care about first.

I look up from pondering what to do about the future of this new timeline, seeing that the rest of the yard is full of delinquents either exercising or talking. Being in the sun is a nice change from being inside, but this was a long enough break. I should get back to my workout.

Where is Angel?

I scan the sea of faces, soon finding he is hanging out with that lanky Hispanic teen from the bathroom fight. They clearly know each other, probably from a prior sentence. They exchange a hand gesture and then disperse into the yard.

Someone falls down, holding their side as blood pours out. People back away, not wanting to be involved.

"Man down! Medic!" I yell as I run to the wounded man. I push people out of the way. It's the lanky Hispanic teen from the bathroom fight.

Multiple stab wounds to the lower right torso. He's breathing isn't compromised, so his lungs are intact. His kidney, stomach, and liver have been punctured. I instinctively reach for my pack, forgetting I don't have it. I'll have to improvise, so I pull off my shirt.

I order, "Move your hands!"

He's panicking, not listening.

I grab his face. "Move your hands, soldier, or I can't stop the bleeding!"

He lifts his hands, and I use my shirt as a makeshift field dressing. The smell of blood hits my nose, and I'm back in the war. I tighten the makeshift bandage, and he winces. "Medic!"

The surrounding delinquents back farther away as guards rush in, pushing them aside. They stare down at me, frozen and unsure what to do with me.

I yell, "Evac now!"

The guards jump into action, and I help them transport the Hispanic teen to the hospital wing. At the door, they tell me to stay, but I don't let go. A guard has to forcibly pull me away and throws me against the wall. I stand there for a minute, looking at my blood-stained hands, then sink down to the ground. What did I just involve myself in? My head hurts, and blood drips from my nose. I just made a huge change to the timeline. I see that Hispanic teen in boot camp, then in the war fighting with us in Baghdad. I see him getting an arm blown off. I see him getting sent home. I see the light of the nuke. He was supposed to die here, and I saved him. I look at the new blood stains on my hands.

"Jason Baker."

I wipe my nose with my sleeve as I stand, smearing it across my face.

Warden Fox is standing above me with a smile, only showing up after everything is over as usual. "I'm very impressed with you, Jason. Your actions just saved David's life. David has been with us for a while and is almost as infamous as you, but for getting in contraband. Saving a fellow delinquent reflects well on you, as well as on all the staff. You should be commended."

This sounds familiar. "No, I didn't do it for medals." I turn away. "If you'll excuse me, I need to clean off this blood."

Warden Fox says, "By all means. Oh, I almost forgot again." He hands me a letter from my family.

I put it in my pocket, not wanting to get any blood on it.

Everyone goes quiet as I walk into B-block. Flashes of more possible futures pop into my head, making me dizzy. I let the blood run down my face, not looking anyone in the eye. In the bathroom, I try to wash the blood off my hands, but it stays under my fingernails. I pick at them, but it won't come off. I look at my face in the mirror. They are the only thing that came with me to this alternate timeline. My eyes have seen too much death. It's nice that my training finally did something positive.

The bathroom door swings open. "Why'd you help him!" There stands Jordan with a four-inch shiv. The original top dog. I've put his position in jeopardy twice now. He stands between me and the door.

I keep my eyes on him in the mirror as I turn off the sink and dry my hands. "It's what I was trained to do. It wouldn't have mattered who was injured. I would have reacted the same." The honest truth, but will he believe me?

He takes a step forward. "You have been nothing but a problem since you got here."

I turn to face him, blood still dripping from my nose.

He's gripping the weapon too tight—a waste of energy.

I can't help but to smile. "You know, it's funny just how easy it is to kill, isn't it?"

He stops four feet from me, just out of striking range.

"It's not even that hard. So many lives taken so easily. Just the pull of a trigger, the push of a button. You tell yourself it's for the right reasons, to protect yourself or the ones you care about. In the end, none of it really matters though. Nothing ever does." I look up at the fluorescent light bulbs, pooling the blood from my nose in the back of my throat. "Death comes for us all." I look him dead in the eyes and spit blood at his face.

The blood splashes in his eyes, and he swings his shiv wildly as he tries to clear his vision.

He yells, "Little bitch!"

That's right, I am little. I use that to my advantage and slip under his arm, then with my full body weight, I kick down on his knee. It cracks inward. I follow the kick with a quick jab to the throat. Unable to scream, he holds his throat as he falls. I stomp on his right arm until he lets go of the shiv, then I grab it and raise it high above him.

An adult voice yells, "Don't do it, Jason!"

It sounds like a guard, but I don't care. I stab down with all of my hate. The cheap metal breaks as it hits the ground next to Jordan's face. I whisper into his ear, "Killing's easy. Living with the consequences is the hard part."

They put me in solitary confinement for being in another fight but only for ten days because I saved David earlier. Jordan will be charged with attempted murder and probably transferred to a maximum security prison, leaving an opening for a new top dog in this place.

Sitting on my lumpy bed, I pull out the crumpled letter from my parents.

Jason, we know you are going through a tough time right now, but we will always be here for you. We know you're not well, and we will do what we can to get you the proper treatment that you need.

Love always, Mom and Dad

It's written on the back of a family photo from the prior Christmas, showing Gramma and Grandpa in hand-knitted sweaters; Uncle Steve with his two sons and soon to be ex-wife, Aunt Margaret; and big brother Pete and big sister Ann smiling for the camera. Then there's little me smiling, showing all my teeth. We all look so happy, but those aren't my eyes anymore.

Tears drip onto the picture. God, I miss them. I miss who I was. I miss the innocence.

When I finally return to my bunk, Angel is reading my notebook. I should have known he would eventually find it. It wasn't that well hidden and he is a lot smarter than he realizes.

He says, "These are some intense notes you have here."

"Yeah."

He says, "They even make sense after a bit."

"Yeah."

He stands up and hands the notebook back to me. "You know David is my cousin. Your one crazy bastard, but thanks for saving his life."

I push the notebook back to him. "I already have it memorized. Want me to show you some of the concepts?"

"Really?" He quickly hides his excitement. "I mean, how did you figure out that the time stream flows through parallel universes?"

"It helps to have seen it." I sit with Angel, explaining the concepts of time and how to travel through it. He listens, holding on to every word. He always did have a thing for math, even if it was just counting cards.

This didn't happen last time. I've never shown Angel the math. I was too afraid he would reject it. Then the strangest thing happens. I don't see any new memories. It's all dark. I still remember all the other memory flashes, but this time, nothing *new* happens.

Angel, *you're* going to save everyone.

CHAPTER 40

FIVE MONTHS LATER, ANGEL IS released. He clutches my notebook as he walks to the bus stop. His father didn't even bother to pick him up. What a dick. I believe in you, my friend. I know you're going to save us all, even if you don't know it yet.

My vision blurs and I try to wipe away my tears, but my eyes are dry. Why is everything suddenly blurry? I keep rubbing my eyes, trying to clear my vision, but nothing is changing.

"W-wha...thaaaa?" My jaw feels wired. I can't move it right. I need some help and try to walk to a guard as my legs start to buckle. My body isn't responding correctly! I hit the ground with a hard thud.

There are no dreams this time. Only the empty black void. It's peaceful here and I want to stay. There's no more fighting. No more anything.

Light starts coming into focus.

No, I don't want to go. I like it here.

My eyes open to a hospital room. I can hear voices and someone crying. What fresh hell am I entering now? I try to get up, but my left side doesn't move. "What the hell?" My mouth is slack, and I can't open my left eye.

I'm hugged by a crying woman.

"Mom?" That's definitely my mother. I'd know her anywhere. "Where am I?" I slur out of a half-controlled mouth.

A doctor comes in with Warden Fox. "Ms. Baker, please let go of the patient. He is in a delicate state."

She doesn't let go.

I hear my father say, "Pete, Ann, can you take your mother out of the room for a second?"

My siblings are here? What the hell is going on? I try to look around the room with only one working eye. The window has bars on it, so I'm still in prison. I watch my older brother and older sister gently help my mother out of the room.

Dad sits down in a chair next to my hospital bed.

The doctor says, "Jason, I have some rather unfortunate news." His voice is hoarse and his posture gives away what he's going to say.

"I'm dying, aren't I?" My voice is cold, lacking all emotion. I'm used to bad news at this point. "Let's just skip the drama and give it to me straight. How long do I have and what's causing it?"

The doctor looks at Warden Fox, horrified by my lack of care.

Warden Fox shrugs in a gesture that says, *I told you so.* "Well, Jason, you have a rather large tumor growing in your brain that caused you to have a stroke."

"And it's attached to the part of my brain that stores my memories. And let me guess, there's too much of a risk to cut it out."

"Well…yes."

The timeline has been severed. This one doesn't need me anymore. With my death, the universe cuts out the anomaly. I knew I wouldn't have a happy ending. That's Pete and Ann's destiny, to have real careers and loving families. I knew that the moment I got the draft letter. I did hold out some hope for something good to come of my life, but that was slowly drained. Angel carries that hope now. All I want now is to protect Luis before my inevitable end.

"A few years at most. You likely won't reach the age of eighteen."

Years? That's not too bad—better than I expected. I had worse odds against the drones. "Should I shave my head, or will you do that for me?"

"We can shave your head, but that's not the treatment you will be receiving."

"I'll be receiving treatment?"

Warden Fox says, "I have already informed your parents. The state is obligated to make sure you survive your sentence. You will receive a form a chemotherapy to prolong your life. We can't cure you."

"Sounds miserable."

I turn to my dad on my left. He's griping my left hand hard, holding back all his pain. It might hurt if my left side wasn't already completely numb.

So that's it, I'm going to die before I turn eighteen. I get to die comfortably in a bed with clean sheets. My brain will deteriorate, and I'll fade back into the darkness. Sounds so peaceful, as well as boring. Just put a bullet through my skull and end it here, save us all the trouble.

Warden Fox and the doctor leave me alone with my

family. I will actually get to say goodbye this time. What should I say? This is so much harder.

I look to my sister, "Ann." My jaw is slowly adjusting to my new way of talking. It ain't perfect, but I can tell she understands me. "You are a beautiful and kind sister. I know you will find someone and make a happy life for yourself. Don't settle for the first because you deserve the best." She tears up but keeps looking at me.

"Pete, you are smart, but don't let that go to your head. You will do great things. Just don't forget about the rest of us."

He says, "Don't you worry about it, little dude. I'll be fine."

"Your sense of danger is lacking. Be careful of certain underage drinking parties." The party we almost got arrested at hasn't happened yet.

"Dad, you are the funniest person I've ever known. Your humor got me through a lot of tough times, more times than you will ever know. Thank you."

He smiles. I know he's trying to think of something funny, but the grief is causing him to draw a blank.

"Mom..." I don't know what to say. There's so much I want to say, but I don't know how. I want to say I'm sorry for all the pain I've caused her, but that won't fix anything. I want to thank her, but how do I express how thankful I am to the woman who brought me into this world. Even though my life was rough, I'm still happy I got to be here for the short time I had.

She hugs me again. "It's ok, Jason. I know."

"I love you, Mom."

Dad joins the hug with Pete and Ann.

"I love you all so much."

CHAPTER 41

THE PAST YEAR HAS BEEN nothing but misery. The drugs have destroyed my body. All my strength has seeped away from me. I'm beginning to look like a living skeleton. However, it hasn't stopped me from pushing myself. I still exercise, but I'm not improving. I get exhausted quicker and quicker. I went from doing a hundred pushups in a day to maybe twenty-five. My left side is even weaker. It took me so long to regain control of it, but it's still not the same. I can't even open my left eye all the way.

I keep pushing myself every day, no matter what. The drugs have destroyed my stomach. I can only eat small amounts of bland paste. My head hurts so much, like I have a permanent migraine. None of the drugs get rid of the pain, only redirect it.

But I can't stop, no matter what. Luis will need me. No matter how sick I feel I have to see the new delinquents. I know one day Luis will be one of them. It's all I strive for now.

One day during my calisthenics, I collapse to the ground after fifteen pushups and am suddenly surrounded by five

Hispanic delinquents. So this is it. I knew it was too good to be true, to die in a comfortable bed.

"We heard the news that you ain't got much time left."

I use all my strength to force myself to my feet. If this is it, I'm not going out easily. "I don't."

I know this guy. What was his name? "You're Angel's cousin, aren't you?"

"David. You saved my life and took down the fucker that stabbed me. I wanted to say thank you before you leave us." He pauses for an awkward amount of time. "So…thank you."

"You're welcome. You hear anything from Angel?"

"His mom took custody, and he's living with her now."

I know nothing about her, but it has to be a better path than before.

They start to leave.

"Wait, David, I need a favor."

"What do you need? I kind of owe you."

"Listen, if a friend of mine ends up here after I'm gone, promise me you'll protect him. His name is Luis and he'll be in for trying to steal a car."

He raises an eyebrow. "An odd favor, but I promise I will."

"Thanks. You have no idea how much weight that take off my shoulders."

CHAPTER 42

FOR SO LONG I HAVE waited. For so long my body has weakened, but finally I see Luis as he's brought in with four others I assume were involved in the robbery.

I can do this. I can protect you.

It doesn't take long until one of the older delinquents confronts Luis, trying to establish he's the top dog. My friend looks so scared.

"Listen here, new meat, you belong to me." The delinquent towers over Luis. Just a mass of pure cut muscle.

I smack the delinquent on his left ass check., "No, he doesn't."

He spins around ready to attack but pauses when he sees my shriveled remains. "If it isn't the dying nut case. Get out of here before I send you to the reaper early."

I know I'm not strong enough to face him head on, but that's why I came prepared. I've already injected him with some of my chemo treatment. That slap was a distraction. It was too easy to get a used syringe from the medical wing. No one pays much attention overnight in the medical wing.

It takes a moment, but he starts to look queasy.

"This is what I have to go through every day. Life is pain and misery, but I can still use the little bit I have left for the right reasons."

He pukes out an undigested breakfast. "What did you do to me, you bastard!" He falls to his knees, clutching his stomach.

I wrap my boney fingers around his neck. "Luis is off limits permanently! Even if I die, my spirit will be here. That is my final curse. Do you understand me?!"

I look over to David and nod.

He nods back. He will do what I can't anymore.

Then I turn to Luis. "Don't worry, buddy. You'll be alright, I promise."

With a look of absolute confusion, Luis says, "Who are you?"

"I'm your friend from another life."

<hr>

Thank you for reading! I hope you enjoyed the story and will stay tuned for the next story in the End of Earth series. Please visit your favorite online retailer and leave a review. I look forward to reading your feedback!

ACKNOWLEDGEMENTS

This book would not have been possible without help from my aunt, Maureen Simons. Thank you for being my first editor and supporting me.

Thank you to my dear friend Cassie. Your input helped me refine the rough edges of the story.

Thank you to Debra L Hartmann for being my editor and helping me publish my first book. I would not have known what to do without you.

Thank you to my good friend Michael Miller as a war adviser. His input and advice from his own war experience helped me tell a more realistic story. Follow him as The Lucky Warlord on Instagram.

A special thank you to my family. Your love and support helped me achieve this accomplishment.

ABOUT THE AUTHOR

 Matt Simons carried the story that would one day become The End of Earth around in his head ever since he was a little kid. The story morphed and evolved through the years, eventually becoming what it is now. All it took was a global pandemic and being trapped in quarantine to start really writing it.

A man with a sense of humor that does not exclude himself, Matt Simons is known among friends and family by his nickname, Nightstand, which he earned while carrying a nightstand down three flights of stairs and across two blocks before realizing it was nearly killing him because it was full of weights. The heavy lesson learned: check the contents of what you will carry around before lifting it.

Let's connect on social media!
Instagram:
https://www.instagram.com/nightstand_matt/
Twitter:
Nightstand Matt at https://twitter.com/MattSim55879370